THE SECRET KEEPERS

THE **SECRET KEEPERS**

Paul Yee

VANCOUVER   LONDON

Distribution and representation in Canada by
Fitzhenry & Whiteside • www.fitzhenry.ca

Distribution and representation in the UK by
Turnaround • www.turnaround-uk.com

Released in the USA in 2012

Mixed Sources
Cert no. SW-COC-001271
© 1996 FSC
FSC
Inside pages printed on FSC certified paper using vegetable-based inks.

Manufactured by Sunrise Printing
Manufactured in Chilliwack, BC, Canada in April 2011

2 4 6 8 10 9 7 5 3 1

Cataloguing-in-Publication Data for this book
is available from The British Library.

Library and Archives Canada Cataloguing in Publication

Yee, Paul
The secret keepers / Paul Yee.

ISBN 978-1-896580-96-8

I. Title.

PS8597.E3S43 2011   jC813'.54   C2010-906149-7

In memory of Garrick Chu and Suzanna Seto

Tradewind Books thanks the Governments of Canada and British Columbia for the financial support they have extended through the Canada Book Fund, Livres Canada Books, the Canada Council for the Arts, the British Columbia Arts Council and the British Columbia Book Publishing Tax Credit program.

**Canada Council
for the Arts**

**Conseil des Arts
du Canada**

BRITISH COLUMBIA
ARTS COUNCIL
Supported by the Province of British Columbia

LIVRES CANADA BOOKS

CHAPTER ONE

April 18, 1906
Wednesday, Early Morning

Pots and pans clattered onto the floor, waking Jackson Leong. He hugged his pillow and cursed the idiot in the kitchen who had disturbed his sweet dream. Then the bells of St. Mary's Church began clanging.

Wallpaper slid by.

Is this a dream? Can the wall be moving?

His bed creaked, scraping against the wall—then shot straight across the room.

"Yahhh!" Jack screamed and covered his eyes.

His older brother, Lincoln, bolted upright. "What's going on?" he shouted.

The two boys hopped out of bed and dashed into Ma's room. She was kneeling next to Anna and Constance, fumbling with their socks and shoes in the dim light of a candle.

Is Ma crazy? Jack wondered. *Taking them for a walk at this hour?*

He flipped the wall switch several times, but there was no electricity.

"Get their coats and take them outside," Ma said.

Jack barely heard her. Now, every church bell in town was ringing: bonging, pealing, tolling and dinging.

"Quick, outside!" Ma shouted. "Earthquake!"

Out front, the San Francisco sky was just brightening. Candles and lanterns bobbed over the street. On one side of the Leongs' nickelodeon was the Tai Hing store and warehouse. Its workers stood on the road, gazing up at the building's third floor. A mound of broken bricks now lay on the ground. Its front wall was completely demolished. The workers jabbered about their good luck, relieved that the fallen wall had not crushed them to death.

On the other side of the nickelodeon, the crew from the Wing Fung Garment Factory argued and cursed as they moved sewing machines onto the street. Ma did piecework for them.

"Stay away from the wall!" hollered Madame Fung, the boss lady. "The earth has not finished shaking yet. There may be aftershocks. And be careful with those machines. We shipped them all the way from New York!"

She wore a stiff blanket over her broad shoulders and red slippers on her feet. Next to her stood Yu-yi, one of her maids.

Her husband, Old Fung, went from worker to worker making sure no one was injured. Usually he wore fashionable

Western suits and leather shoes, but now his bare feet and baggy pyjamas made him look like a scarecrow.

Ma came running out. Her long skirt swirled behind her. "The roof may collapse!" she cried, blocking Lincoln's way.

"I have to save the projector!" he yelled. "And the movies! We still owe money to the bank."

Every two weeks, the Edison Company sent out new films while Lincoln forwarded the old ones to the next theatre on the circuit. *The Great Train Robbery*, *Life of an American Fireman* and *The Ex-Convict* were still inside the nickelodeon. Lincoln had bragged to Jack about his great plans for the business. He was sure that he could become a millionaire by showing movies in China.

Ma dragged Lincoln away from the building. He was sixteen, but she treated him like a five-year-old. He was big and tall and had quickly learned everything the family needed to know about their new hometown. But that didn't matter. Ma had the final say on everything.

Jack crept to the window and looked inside. Miraculously the projector, the piano and the chairs and benches were undamaged. Nothing had fallen over.

"Get away from the building!" Ma called out. "Go take care of your sisters."

"Bring the crates into the middle of the road," Madame Fung ordered Yu-yi.

"Let me help you," Lincoln said.

He's soft on Yu-yi, Jack thought.

"Sit!" Madame Fung said with a nervous laugh, turning to Ma. "When the Earth Dragon moves again, it's better to feel the tremors on our cushy bums."

"If only Ba hadn't died," Ma said, "then we'd be safe in Marysville on the farm. And if Gee Uncle hadn't gone to China, then he'd be here to take care of us."

"The telephone exchange is down," Old Fung blurted. "There's no water. The gas lines are leaking. Don't light matches. Don't smoke. The whole city might explode."

Jack's cousin Kern ran up, breathless. He was Lincoln's age, and bigger and taller than Jack. "The city is in ruins!" he shouted. "This is the biggest disaster ever!"

The two boys darted up California Street. A crowd of dazed-looking people stared down the slope toward the harbour at the dark black smoke rising from raging fires. Usually at this time of the day, San Francisco's thick fog shrouded the downtown core, hiding everything except the upper windows of the tallest towers.

Buildings and walls had collapsed along the steep hillside near the boys. Homes were slashed open like dollhouses, exposing fireplaces, chairs and paintings. People dragged furniture onto the sidewalk.

Suddenly the cobblestones under the boys' feet shuddered.

"Earthquake!" Kern shouted, grabbing Jack.

"Let go!"

A fire wagon clattered past with horses galloping at full speed.

A man rushed through the crowd, pulling a baby carriage that clinked and clanked with the brittle sound of chinaware. A cage holding a squawking blue-green parakeet rested on top. It sounded like a frightened child.

People are crazy, Jack thought. *They're saving dishes?*

Two men carried a woman out of a nearby house. Her long nightdress was soaked in blood. They laid her on the sidewalk, covered her with heavy blankets and bent over her. One man pulled her hand to his lips.

Jack saw the woman's ghost rise up through the blankets and float over the houses. It drifted away without looking back. Both of the men howled in grief when they realized the woman had died.

Today is going to be bad, very bad. Ghosts will be everywhere! I wish I didn't have yin-yang eyes. Jack turned away, feeling sick. He had never let anyone, not even Lincoln, find out about his ability to see ghosts, because he knew people would avoid him like a bad disease.

Gusts of acrid smoke suddenly engulfed them.

"We'd better run!" Kern said, coughing like a sick man. "The fires are coming this way!"

The boys hurried back to the nickelodeon.

Ma was still chatting with Madame Fung. "Do you think it's safe to go to the temple?" Ma asked, holding Constance on her lap while Anna clung to her skirt.

"I hope so. We need to pray. Offerings at the temple go straight to the gods."

Yung Uncle ran up, all out of breath. He was still neatly dressed in a cook's uniform for his job at a fancy downtown hotel.

"What are you waiting for?" he shouted to everyone, jumping onto a crate. "Run! Hoodlums are looting downtown shops. Entire streets are burning. The army is there! The fire is spreading! Get out of Chinatown; otherwise you'll burn to death!"

Ma began to weep, which started the girls whimpering.

"I'd better find the old ones," Kern said, rushing off down the street.

Lincoln gestured to Jack. "This way—hurry!"

The boys ran behind the nickelodeon. Lincoln grabbed an old wheelbarrow that had lain upside down ever since the family had moved in. Its rusty wheels squealed, refusing to turn. The brothers pushed and heaved it up the back stairway. Finally, it slid over the threshold.

"Help me get the projector," Lincoln said, heading into the nickelodeon.

They lifted the projector onto the wheelbarrow and cushioned it with blankets.

"What about the piano?" Jack asked.

"Don't be silly, you idiot. It's too big."

Outside, Kern's parents, Cat Uncle and Cat Aunty, had arrived. Although Cat Aunty and Ma were sisters, they looked very different. Ma's face was brown and weathered, and her body was sturdy from years of doing farm work, while her sister was a city lady, pale and delicate. Ma always wore Western-style skirts and boots, while Cat Aunty shimmered in embroidered silks. But today Cat Aunty wore a long coat and hat instead of Chinese clothes.

"I told you not to go inside!" Ma scolded the boys. "You could have been hurt!"

"We're fine," Lincoln insisted. "Stop worrying!"

"Can I help you with that wheelbarrow?" Cat Uncle asked.

"I could push this thing all the way to New York with one hand!"

"Don't worry. Everything will turn out all right," Cat Uncle said to Ma.

She didn't answer. Ma kept her distance from Cat Uncle because he ran an opium shop. Even so, Cat Aunty was close to Ma and often babysat her nieces.

"You should have gone to China with Gee Uncle," Cat Aunty said.

Gee Uncle was Ba's brother, the other side of the family.

"You know we couldn't. He insisted that Lincoln run the nickelodeon," Ma said, wiping her eyes.

"The fire is coming closer and burning everything in its path!" Old Fung yelled. "Get out of Chinatown now!"

Lincoln tied Constance onto Jack's back, and she held tightly onto a fistful of his hair. Jack took Anna's hand and they set off behind Lincoln, who was pushing the wheelbarrow.

"Did you bring anything to eat?" Anna asked.

Jack shook his head.

They hurried up California Street. A warm gritty wind blew up from the bay. The street swarmed with people fleeing the flames. Everybody shouted advice. Strangers helped one another. Nob Hill was steep, and there was rubble from fallen buildings everywhere. Deep potholes cratered the ground. The cable car rail that ran straight up and down the hill was now bent and crooked.

Jack had never seen such a massive crowd. People were weighed down by bulging carpet bags. They dragged children clutching precious toys. Men and boys pushed wagons filled with furniture.

When a carriage pulled by, some people called out asking for a ride. Cat Uncle's family pressed ahead, leaving Ma and the children behind.

Shouldn't we all stay together? Jack thought. *If Ma were nicer to Cat Uncle, he would wait for us to catch up.*

"Watch the girls closely!" Ma yelled as she was swept away by a surge of the crowd.

"Hold on tight, Connie," Jack said. She grabbed his shirt collar, and he squeezed Anna's sticky hand.

"What happened there?" Anna asked, pointing to a brass bed dangling out of a second-floor window, its bedsheet flapping in the wind. "And there!" A bedroom mirror taller than Lincoln was snagged in the high branches of a tree.

Anna looked at everything. Every stained-glass window, gold-painted sign and black iron railing caught her eye.

"Who did that?" she asked, pointing at a gleaming white bathtub, lying on its side.

How can I explain this to her? Jack thought.

Dogs were running wild, barking at everyone. Their owners had probably left them behind.

"Where are we going?" Anna asked.

Jack wanted to shrug, but he caught himself and comforted her by saying, "We're going back to our old farm in Marysville."

A second later, she repeated her question.

"Don't you believe me?" Jack snapped. "You always believe Lincoln."

Jack hated San Francisco. It rained too much. His one set of clothes stayed damp for days. Kern was his only real friend. School was painful. After classes he went home right away because Ma worried that he might get beaten or stabbed or tossed into the bay by white hooligans. She wouldn't let Anna go out to play in the streets by herself, because Ma was afraid she'd be kidnapped. Jack wanted to go back to the farm.

Now we have a perfect excuse to leave the city for good.

"I want Mama!" Anna whined.

Jack looked around but couldn't see Ma or Lincoln anywhere. He dragged Anna up the stairs of a nearby house to get a better view. A river of frightened people streamed toward them: white and black and brown faces, young and old, some well-dressed and others not. But there was no one he knew.

They must be ahead of us.

Jack yanked Anna down to the street and told her to walk faster. She whimpered and threatened to throw a tantrum.

Doesn't she know we're in the middle of an earthquake, and the city is breaking apart!

"Jackson! Jackson!" Lincoln shouted.

Jack stood on his tiptoes and saw his brother waving in the midst of the crowd, but a mob of panicky, shouting people suddenly blocked them.

"Elder Brother is coming!" Jack told Anna. "He'll carry you so you don't have to walk."

Jack and his sisters struggled through the wall of people toward Lincoln, but his brother had disappeared from sight. He heard people yelling and then a loud crash.

When he finally got closer, he saw a wagon overturned on the road. Heavy furniture was scattered everywhere. A hand and shirt sleeve poked out from under the overturned wagon.

"No," he gasped. *It's Lincoln!*

Madame Fung's maid, Yu-yi, stood next to the overturned wagon. She was weeping.

"A runaway wagon rolled down the hill and hit him," Old Fung said, patting Jack's shoulder. "It looks bad."

Madame Fung sat in her buggy holding her head in her hands.

"Get out of the way!" someone shouted at Old Fung.

Old Fung quickly lifted Yu-yi onto the buggy next to the sewing machines and bundles of cloth. Then he clucked at his horse and urged it forward.

At that moment Lincoln's ghost rose up from the overturned wagon and floated away, his head tilted toward the sky.

Farewell, Elder Brother. Take care of yourself.

"Jack, Anna!"

He looked around. Ma was pushing the wheelbarrow through the onlookers. When she saw Jack's stricken face and the shirt sleeve under the wagon, she screamed and fell forward. Weeping and moaning, she crawled to Lincoln. Jack knelt and pulled the girls close so they wouldn't see Ma. Anna and Constance were crying, and Jack couldn't see for the tears in his eyes. He murmured his brother's name. He felt people walk by, heard them murmur and mutter, and smelled the pungent horse dung on the road.

What would they do now?

He stood up. Ma's face was tear-stained, her eyes swollen and red.

"What do we do?" Jack asked. "We can't leave him lying there. We'll have to push him all the way across town!"

"That's right." Ma snapped. "Lift him into the wheelbarrow. We can't stay here."

"What about the projector?"

Just then, uniformed soldiers came by with a wagon piled high with bodies, some wrapped in blankets.

"Stand aside," a soldier said. "We'll take care of him."

Two of them pulled Lincoln out from under the overturned wagon and swung his body on top of the others.

"Wait!" Ma shouted at the soldiers. Then she stepped up to the wagon and tapped Lincoln's shoulder.

"To send him on his way," she said, looking at Jack. "Let's go, now. We have to keep moving."

She tied a cord around Anna's wrist and fastened it to her belt. "Lift Constance onto my back."

Jack wanted to ask about burying Lincoln and about what rituals to perform. Instead he kept silent, focusing on pushing the wheelbarrow to the top of Nob Hill. At the top loomed the castle-like Fairmont Hotel, so new that it wasn't even open yet. Somehow it had withstood the earthquake with little damage.

The family flowed with the crowd, trudging across the city, past streets and houses they had never seen before. From time to time, Jack looked behind him. Huge dark clouds boiled in the sky.

It's the end of the world. I wonder how many people died today.

Later that afternoon the family reached Golden Gate Park. Soldiers were busy putting up canvas tents for the thousands of refugees. Horses and wagons clattered by.

Ma sank down on the grass, and Jack untied Constance.

"Go walk around," Ma said, "and look for Chinese people."

Jack's feet ached, yet off he went. Every few steps he glanced back. It wasn't long before trees and people swallowed up Ma, the wheelbarrow and his sisters.

"Make way! Make way!" Soldiers rushed by with a body on a stretcher. Other uniformed men drove metal spikes into the ground to erect tents. Babies wailed. Teams of horses trotted by. People carried pails of precious water. Old people sat on the grass, dazed, staring at the ground. Children chased each other, playing games and laughing as if they were on a picnic. Jack didn't see any Chinese people, but he kept on walking. Near some trees, a man embraced a sobbing woman. Someone opened an umbrella and held it over them.

Jack gave up, turned around and tried to find his way back. But he had no idea which direction to take. Every tent looked the same.

He felt a hand on his shoulder. It was Kern and Cat Uncle.

"Where's your mother?" Cat Uncle asked. "We've been looking for you everywhere."

"At the entrance to the park, but I don't know the way back."

"Hey, what's wrong with your face?" Kern asked. "Have you been crying?"

"Lincoln was killed."

Silently, Cat Uncle shook his head and put his arm around Jack.

After a while Jack asked, "What rituals should we do for Lincoln? At Ba's funeral, we had black arm bands for everyone, plenty of incense, offerings of ghost money and bowing to his portrait."

"We do not do anything for Lincoln," Cat Uncle said softly.

"Because of the earthquake?"

"Because your mother is still alive. A child should not die before his parents. It is not the way of the universe. Therefore, when such a terrible thing happens, we ignore it."

"Then we'll forget all about Lincoln!" Jack exclaimed. "That's not right."

CHAPTER TWO

November 1907
Sunday Evening

"**N**o other fifteen-year-old in San Francisco gets to run a nickelodeon!" Cat Uncle exclaimed, clapping Jack on the shoulder. "You are the luckiest boy in the world! Congratulations on your grand opening!"

"Seedless plums—your favourite!" Kern shoved a paper bundle at his cousin. "Hope you make lots of money!"

Jack grinned and showed them to the best seats in the house.

Before Gee Uncle left for China, he had asked Old Bread-face to help Lincoln. And after the earthquake and Lincoln's death, it was Old Bread-face who suggested that the family borrow money from the bank to rebuild the nickelodeon. He promised to help Jack run it, and assured Ma that they would make enough to pay back the loan in a year.

Ma had said that as soon as that was done and they made a healthy profit, the family would sail to China. But that was the last place in the world Jack wanted to go. Ghosts from hundreds of years of history haunted China. He would see them everywhere. China had no electricity to light up the nights and repel ghosts. Jack shuddered as he recalled the spooky stories he had heard the Chinese workers tell when they sat outside to cool off on hot summer nights at Ba's farm.

As customers poured into the nickelodeon, loud voices and laughter filled the hall. Everyone praised the new building.

"Look how solid those beams and trusses are!" a man in overalls exclaimed.

"Everything is safer than before the earthquake," another man added.

Jack would never admit it aloud, but he was scared. He wasn't ready to step into Lincoln's shoes and run the business.

Something is bound to go wrong tonight, and I'll end up looking stupid in front of everyone.

Jack admired the way Old Bread-face welcomed people at the door and shook their hands. He knew everyone's name, made them laugh at his jokes and talked them out of getting their change back. He never wore suits like Ba or Uncle Gee, but tonight he looked quite smart in a Western shirt, jacket and tie. Although each piece of clothing was a different colour and nothing matched, Jack felt shabby in comparison.

The customers didn't pay any attention to Jack, much less shake his hand. With Lincoln, they had acted very differently. They would always greet him warmly and invite him along for a meal and drinks while Jack fumed with jealousy. Later, when he asked his brother what they had talked about, Lincoln said he told them funny stories about life on the farm. But he never told Jack any stories like that.

"Boy, has your mother finished yesterday's piecework?" Old Fung asked Jack.

"No, she's still not well."

Cat Aunty had found sewing jobs for Ma to do at home, so she could support the family while the nickelodeon got off the ground after Ba's death. But lately she had been too sick to finish the work on time.

"My wife just came back from China," Old Fung said. "Tell your mother to come for a visit."

"Where's the toilet?" a fat sweaty man demanded.

"Outside, sir," Jack replied, pointing over his shoulder.

"Not inside?"

"The plumbing isn't finished yet."

"In my new factory," Old Fung said smugly, "we installed the toilets before anything else. That way, we made sure the workers were happy." Then he strode away.

The backyard had been lit with gas lanterns to help people get to the toilet. Long ago, Gee Uncle had joked about a ghost haunting the outhouse, but Jack had never seen one there. Whenever people told Jack that a place was haunted, it never was. They didn't have yin-yang eyes like he did; they were just scared or superstitious. Even so, Jack avoided the outhouse just in case.

"Hello, William Uncle." Jack greeted the piano player. He wasn't a relative, but Jack showed respect by addressing him properly.

When William Uncle played the piano, he didn't need any sheet music. His fingers danced over the keyboard as if they had a mind of their own. Old Bread-face said it was fortunate that William Uncle had come back to San Francisco after surviving the earthquake. Not everyone had returned.

"*Wah*, big crowd!" William Uncle exclaimed. "Hope they stay for the second show!"

"Jackson!" Old Bread-face yelled. "Get over here!"

George and Albert, Jack's worst enemies, loitered at the door. They wore knee pants and long stockings just like Jack, but their leather boots gleamed from polishing. They had servants at home—that was why. At school they bullied Jack by hiding his cap and leading the class in chanting, "Jackass Jack, Jackass Jack, Jackass Jack."

Jack tried to get back at them by yanking their queues any chance he got.

"These monkeys say you promised to let them in for free," Old Bread-face said. "Is that true?"

Jack nodded. His face reddened.

"Told you so!" the bullies shouted, marching away and laughing.

"Our bank loan will not get paid off that way," Old Bread-face muttered.

True, Jack thought, *but* you *don't have to face George and Albert every day.*

Old Bread-face signalled Jack to start the projector as soon as the lights went out. Jack gulped and wiped his sweaty palms on his pants. The films had arrived late, and there hadn't been time for a practice run. He was worried that the projector might have been damaged when the family had camped for several damp nights in Golden Gate Park.

As Jack flipped the lamp and motor switches, William Uncle played an upbeat tune. The film reels spun and whirred, throwing moving pictures onto the taut white sheet stretched across the front of the room. A sunlit meadow appeared, and a horse galloped by, pulling a buggy that teetered dangerously. People gasped in awe at the magic in front of them.

The first film was *Catch the Kid*—a comedy—and the audience laughed loudly. For a moment, Jack felt confident that the nickelodeon would become a big success.

"Ghost!" Temple Keeper shouted, jumping in front of the projector and blocking the screen. "I saw a ghost!" He pointed to the corner of the room.

Jack turned and saw a woman's face flicker there and then disappear. A chill went up his back.

The audience leaped to their feet and stampeded out of the hall and into the night.

"Stop!" Old Bread-face shouted in vain. "Calm down! Someone will get hurt!"

"I felt a tingle on my neck," William Uncle said.

"No wonder it was cold in there," Old Bread-face muttered.

The ceiling lights flickered on. Chairs and benches were knocked upside down, and bags of peanuts and sunflower seeds had been spilled all over the floor.

Jack saw the ghost again. She was wearing a Chinese blue smock and floated in front of the sheet, shaking her head in disapproval. Jack could see right through her. He panicked and dashed outside, breaking free of the crowd.

He ran past apartment blocks and construction sites with wooden frames and half-finished buildings. He ran past ramshackle shacks and makeshift tents. One house smelled strongly of fresh paint. Finally he stopped at a corner with a streetlamp to catch his breath.

Bad, very bad. Now we'll never pay off the bank loan.

Someone grabbed his shoulder. Jack jumped and yelped.

"Jack, you scream like a girl!" Kern whooped and laughed so hard that he bent over.

"*Wooooo*," he shrieked, holding his hands like claws and slashing them around. "I'm the ghost! Run, Jackson, run!"

"You didn't see the ghost, did you? Why did you run?" asked Jack.

"Hey, if Temple Keeper said he saw a ghost, then there must have been a ghost."

Everyone in Chinatown knew that Temple Keeper's yin-yang eyes saw phantoms and spirits. That was why he had been chosen to maintain the altars and accept the offerings from worshippers. He earned a living telling people's fortunes and selling anti-ghost charms. But Temple Keeper always ate alone in restaurants. Nobody wanted to sit with him; everyone was afraid he attracted ghosts. Jack just wanted to be normal.

"Let me buy you noodles," Kern said. "How about roast duck?"

"Where'd you get the money?"

"From my mother."

"Really?"

"Of course! Coming?"

"Sure."

There was nothing shiny or colourful about Golden Chrysanthemum Garden because it was just a large shed thrown together from odd pieces of new and second-hand lumber. But its racks of sweet-smelling roast meats fed hungry customers all day long, while the steam from its bubbling cauldrons of boiling broth warmed those who were cold. Jack and Kern slurped at their noodles and drank every last drop of soup.

After the waiter took the dishes away, Kern grinned. "I've got a plan."

"Not another one!" Jack groaned.

"This one will work, for sure. And you're going to need money now. No one will go back to your nickelodeon after word gets around about the ghost."

"What's your plan?"

"We break into the Chinese Methodist Church tonight and steal the offering money. It's Sunday so they won't have had a chance to deposit it in the bank."

"Not a good idea. Not after we just got visited by a ghost."

"Is it bad luck?"

"Yeah, sure is. Not only that, the ghost could be following us."

"How would you know?" Kern's gaze darted around. "Is there one here?"

"Don't believe me if you don't want. But why take the chance?"

"Then what do you want to do now?"

"Go home."

Jack paused before opening his apartment door.

How am I going to tell Ma about the ghost? What if she faints and falls to the ground and gets sicker?

When he got inside, Ma was still up, sewing.

"How are you feeling?" Jack asked.

"A little better. Were there lots of customers?" she asked.

"Yes, but when the lights went out, Temple Keeper jumped up and shouted that he saw a ghost. Everyone ran."

"It must have been Lincoln!" Ma exclaimed.

Jack knew it wasn't, but he didn't answer. Instead he went into the kitchen and poked around for some food. He was still hungry, even after the roast duck. He found leftover rice, cold sausage and soggy leaves of bok choy. His mother stood by the door.

"Your brother is angry and blames me for his death. He was too young to die. It's my fault."

"Ma, Lincoln died in an accident. There wasn't anything you could do about it."

"No, it was my fault," she insisted. "When I saw you and Anna and Constance on the other side of the road, I should have gone to fetch you myself. But I sent Lincoln instead."

Jack filled his mouth with food.

I wish I could tell her that the ghost I just saw was a woman. That would stop her from blaming herself. But if I tell her, then she'll know about my yin-yang eyes.

Without knocking, Old Bread-face stomped through the front door. His face was red with fury. "Where did you run off to, stupid boy? The customers came back and wanted refunds. It was madness! I was surrounded. You were supposed to be helping me!"

"There was a ghost!"

"Lincoln would not have been afraid," Old Bread-face said.

"Lincoln's ghost must have come back," Ma said, twisting a dishcloth in her hands.

"Why would he harm his own family? Lincoln loved the nickelodeon."

"You don't think the ghost was Lincoln? Who else could it be?"

"It could be anyone, maybe someone who died in the earthquake," Jack said.

Old Bread-face threw his hands up and thumped around the room. "Your two no-use friends from school demanded their money back. What nerve—after you let them in for free! Do they think I am stupid?"

"What will we do now, close the hall?" asked Ma.

"Close? How can we close?" Old Bread-face asked. "We have to make payments to the bank. If we miss just one of them, they will take our building!"

"But customers won't come to a haunted hall," Jack said.

"This is what we do. Tomorrow, you go see Temple Keeper. I would go myself, but I have to tend to my store. Ask him if he knows who the ghost is, what it wants and if he can give us a charm to keep the ghost away. I will pay for whatever it costs."

Then he said goodnight to Ma, put his cap on his head and hurried off.

"But . . . what if it is Lincoln's ghost?" Ma asked, her voice cracking.

"Ma, Old Bread-face ruled that out! Didn't you hear? Besides, Lincoln wouldn't do anything to hurt us."

"I'm his mother. I should have protected him, kept him safe

from accidents and death. That's what parents are supposed to do."

Constance started crying in the other room and Ma hurried to her.

Jack gazed out the window. In the distance, electric lights glowed in the upper floor windows of downtown buildings. The Spreckels Tower dominated the skyline, standing nineteen storeys high with a fancy domed top. It had survived the earthquake and fire along with the grandiose Flood and Kohl buildings. Kern had told him that only three months after the earthquake, eighteen of the city's biggest buildings had been repaired and were open for business.

With every ounce of his being, Jack wished that Ba and Lincoln were still alive. Then they would be taking care of Ma and him and his sisters. Now, with them gone, all the responsibility for the family had landed on him. He had no idea how to look after them properly.

I'm not ready for all this.

CHAPTER THREE

Monday Morning

"**G**host-boy, ghost-boy, don't come around. Ghost-boy, ghost-boy, stay underground!"

Jack's classmates, boys and girls alike, were chanting as he entered the classroom. When he sat down, everyone who had desks near him jumped up and ran off to sit somewhere else.

"Look! The ghost is on his shoulder," one boy whispered.

"Watch out! It crawled into his desk!" said another.

Jack opened his book and pretended to read.

Ghost-boy? Hah! Doesn't bother me. It's better than Jackass!

"Ghost-boy, ghost-boy, don't come around. Ghost-boy, ghost-boy, stay underground!"

Mrs. Newhall, the principal, walked in, picked up a metal

ruler and slammed it on the desk. Everyone froze.

"This class is getting detention! Miss Strickland is sick today, so I'll be taking over the class. Take out your grammar books."

When the lunch bell rang, Jack ran for the door. Outside, Albert stuck out a foot. Jack went flying and bounced off a railing. He grimaced in pain as everyone laughed. Then Jack jumped up and grabbed Albert by the neck. But two other boys yanked Jack's arms behind his back. They held him as Albert slapped Jack's face, right to left, then left to right, over and over.

"Not fair!" he shouted, struggling to get free. "Five against one!"

"So get a friend to help you," sneered Albert. "If you have any!"

The boys laughed and started chanting again. "Ghost-boy, ghost-boy, doesn't have a friend!"

If Kern hadn't been expelled last term for rubbing their faces in mud puddles, then for sure he would take care of them.

Jack kicked at Albert, who danced out of the way.

"Stop it!" Mrs. Newhall shouted, rushing over.

When Jack reached home, the door to the apartment was slightly open, and he heard voices coming from the sitting room. He slipped inside and saw Yu-yi move over to sit on the low stool right next to Ma.

"I saw Lincoln last night," Yu-yi said in a small voice.

Another ghost? Jack shuddered and peeked into the room.

"My son?" Ma dropped the sock she was darning and grabbed Yu-yi's wrist. "Where? Where did you see him?"

"At the store, in a mirror in a darkened room."

"Are you sure it was him?"

"Of course! Oh, I'm so scared, Mrs. Leong. Please help me! I did wrong and I know it!"

"Wrong? What wrong?" Ma sounded anxious.

Jack moved closer to hear better.

"Please, don't get angry," Yu-yi said in a tearful voice.

"No use crying if you did wrong."

"I know."

"Tell me what happened. I won't scold you."

There was a pause before Yu-yi spoke. "I used to look forward to the days when Lincoln came to fetch or deliver your piecework. Those were the happiest moments in my life! We always glanced at each other. He would try to stay as long as he could. Then one day he gave me this."

"His birthday handkerchief!" Ma gasped. "I spent hours stitching his initials onto it. Then he told me he lost it. I was furious!"

"Nothing happened between us." Yu-yi sobbed. "I swear to the gods above, nothing! We barely spoke two words to each other!"

"I don't believe you."

"We had no time to do anything. Lincoln died in the earthquake."

"Why are you telling me all this?" Ma's voice was cold now.

"I fear Lincoln's ghost. I went to ask Temple Keeper for

a protective charm, but he won't help me unless I pay him. Please, Missus, can you lend me some cash?"

"I can't spare anything! I have three children to feed and the rent to pay! Ask Madame Fung for the money!"

"That's the last thing she will do. She's trying to get rid of me! She and Dolly Aunty have arranged for me to marry your landlord Old Kong. I told them that I would kill myself before taking him for my husband."

She's my age! Jack gasped. *How can she marry someone so old?*

"Ah, now I know what is going on!" Ma exclaimed. "Yu-yi, Lincoln wants you to be his ghost bride."

"Ghost bride?" Yu-yi's voice squeaked, sounding shakier than before.

"Young men who die without a wife are doomed to wander alone in the afterlife," Ma explained. "Sometimes, their families will match them to young girls who died unmarried. Other times, the young man may come back seeking a wife from the living world."

Yu-yi gasped. "I'm doomed." But then her voice changed. "Why, Lincoln thinks he's saving me from marrying Old Kong! When I first saw him in the mirror, his hands kept beckoning me closer. But my feet were frozen, and I couldn't move. I want to stay in the world of the living. Please, Missus, help me. I'm too scared to sleep at night."

"Don't worry. Jack is going to see Temple Keeper. He'll get you an anti-ghost charm."

"Will that be enough?"

"Of course. Temple Keeper has very powerful skills."

"But you said you couldn't spare any money."

"I'm Lincoln's mother. I'm still responsible for him."

"Oh, thank you, Missus."

When Yu-yi reached the door, her eyes widened as she spotted Jack. Her mouth opened, but Jack quickly put a finger to his lips.

"Shush," he whispered, letting her out and slamming the door. Then he called out, "Ma, I'm home. Is there anything to eat?"

Right after the earthquake, the army had marched into Chinatown and dynamited the buildings to stop the fires from spreading. Before soldiers reached the temple, however, devoted followers had carried away the sacred flame as well as the statues of the gods. Since then, a makeshift temple had been constructed on the original site. Jack had heard people grumbling about the builder, who had not cut any windows or installed any glass in the walls in order to save money. From the outside, the building hardly looked like a sacred place.

The temple interior was dim, lit only by candles. The gods sat on high altars that were covered with brocades. In the dim light, smoky wisps rose from a brass cauldron filled with fragrant incense. Scrolls and colourful tapestries, gifts from grateful worshippers, hung on the walls.

Jack walked softly to avoid disturbing the gods.

I've got to be strong here; otherwise I won't lose my fear of ghosts.

"What do you want, boy?" a voice called from the shadows.

Jack bristled. *Who's he calling "boy"?*

"Oh, it's you!" Temple Keeper said, stepping out of the darkness.

He did not have wrinkled skin and long white whiskers like the temple guardian in Marysville. He was youthful, with a clean-shaven face and bright eyes. His dark shirt fit him snugly, and he looked like any other worker in Chinatown.

"I was expecting you, but not so soon. I just came back from digging up bones to send back to China. Tell me, does that frighten you?"

Jack pushed his shoulders back. "I'm not scared of bones, sir," he said, trying to sound polite and respectful.

"But you fear ghosts, do you not?"

Jack was taken aback.

"I saw you run away from the nickelodeon with all the other spineless fools."

"That ghost you saw, sir, was it a man or a woman?"

"Why do you ask?"

"My mother thinks it's my brother's spirit. He died in the earthquake."

"No. I saw a woman."

"Who was she?"

"I did not recognize her."

"What does she want?"

Temple Keeper frowned and turned away. "I don't know," he said irritably, "but she must have unfinished business, or else she wouldn't have come back to haunt the nickelodeon. You'd better find out what she wants and give it to her. Only then will she leave you alone."

"Old Bread Face wants you to do something."

"I can go to your movie hall and conduct a ritual to drive

away the ghost. You won't be able to reopen until I perform a ritual. People will be too scared to go there and sit in the dark to watch movies."

"How much will that cost?"

"Ten dollars."

"So much? What about a charm?"

"Which sort do you want?" When Jack shrugged his shoulder Temple Keeper snorted and started to pace back and forth. "There are many different types. I can make you one to wear, to protect yourself, or I can write a wall charm that you put up to keep ghosts out of your home. I can write it on paper or on cloth. And if you knew who was haunting you, I could write a charm to protect you from that one ghost. Each charm comes with a different price."

Jack pulled at Temple Keeper's arm. "Yu-yi, Madame Fung's servant girl, came to you about my brother's ghost. My mother wants to give her a charm, to stop Lincoln from harming her."

Temple Keeper shook his head. "I don't know what that girl saw. She was so scared she could barely talk."

"Can you make an anti-ghost charm for her?"

"Of course."

"Then add it to our bill."

By late afternoon the overnight fog had lifted. Jack trudged up the steep hill that led home, past work crews clambering up ladders and installing windows. The sounds of hammering and sawing filled the air. There was so much construction underway in Chinatown that it was never quiet, not until dusk. Nearby, downtown office buildings sprouted up that were bigger and taller than those from before the earthquake.

A brisk wind whipped across Jack's face and reminded him of the flat farmlands in Marysville. After Ba's death, when Ma had refused to cook and the farm was falling apart, Jack had often gone to the cemetery. Those were the only times he had ever longed to see a ghost. But Ba had never shown up.

Jack was seven years old the first time he saw a ghost. Ba and Ma had taken the horse and wagon into town early in the morning and had returned late that afternoon. While Ma scrambled to cook the evening meal for the farmhands, Jack noticed a guest in the sitting room—a gentleman in a dark suit and tie. He wore a fedora and had well-polished shoes. He sat quietly on their one good chair.

The family usually ate in the kitchen, apart from the workers. But if the Leongs had visitors, they used the dining room. It was Jack's turn to set the table. Because there was a guest, he opened the dining room table and put out an extra setting. He expected Ma to compliment him for doing so without needing to be told.

When Ma saw the dining table set with extra chopsticks, she grabbed Jack. "Why did you set the big table?"

"For our guest."

"What guest?"

Jack led her into the sitting room. The man was still there but had fallen asleep.

"There's nobody here!" Ma exclaimed. "Are you playing a joke on me?"

A week later, one of the farmhands mentioned to Jack that his parents had attended a funeral that day. Jack never told anyone, not even Lincoln, about the man in the sitting room. But he saw many more ghosts after that.

At the apartment block, he found Old Kong waiting in the front hall. It looked as if the landlord had been squatting on the stairs for a while, because the floor was littered with toothpicks. A strong tobacco odour hung around him as well.

"Where's the rent? It's a week overdue," Old Kong said, spitting out a toothpick.

"Sir, as soon as the nickelodeon reopens, you'll get the money."

"Can't your mother borrow money from your aunty? Cat King is a rich man!"

"You know my mother would never do that! She refuses to touch Cat Uncle's money."

"This is no time to be fussy! I don't run a charity. I have expenses: electricity, water, taxes, insurance. Look around. San Francisco is filled with people walking the streets with their suitcases and hunting for places to rent."

"I promise, you'll get your money."

"Rent in full within a week. Otherwise I'll kick you out!"

As Old Kong went out the front door, he passed Cat Uncle. The two men grunted at each other. Jack greeted his uncle politely and then blurted out, "Uncle, can you give me a job?"

"What?" Then he lowered his voice. "You know your mother would never let that happen."

"Our rent is overdue. We need money."

Cat Uncle shook his head. "Cat Aunty won't even let Kern work for me."

"She's afraid Kern will get arrested by the police," said Jack. "Aren't you?"

"I have no choice." Jack put on a brave front, even though the thought of landing behind iron bars made him shudder.

"Will you tell your mother?"

"Of course not."

"You'd better not. I don't want her shouting at me, saying that I led my nephew astray and ruined his life."

"I promise."

"All right, then."

"When do I start?"

"Tomorrow night."

Finally, I'm doing something useful!

CHAPTER FOUR

Tuesday, After School

Old Bread-face pulled Jack along, forcing him to march at double speed along the street.

"What's wrong?" Jack demanded.

"Temple Keeper is performing a ritual at the nickelodeon. You are the owner. You need to be there."

Oh no, not more ghosts!

"What about you? You're the one who's paying."

"Of course I'll be there."

"Will this take long? I have to help Ma. And I have homework."

"You're not afraid of ghosts, are you?"

"No!"

"Liar! You ran away from the hall the other night. You need to grow up."

That stung. Jack pulled away, but Old Bread-face didn't slow down. He didn't even look back at Jack.

When the cable car whizzed by, clanging its bell, Jack felt like jumping aboard and riding far away. When he'd first arrived in San Francisco, he had thought the cars were magical. There was nothing pushing or pulling them as they climbed smoothly up and down the steep hills all day long. Then Kern explained that two thick cables clattered along under the tracks, one going up, another going down. Inside each car, the driver gripped the cable when he wanted to go forward, and then let go of it when he wanted to stop. It was so simple that Jack had slapped his head.

Temple Keeper looked powerful and mysterious, like a warrior armed with supernatural weapons. He wore a yellow robe that reached down to the floor. Its flowing sleeves billowed out. A box-like black helmet with a square of gleaming jade in its centre sat on his head. Jack backed away, but Old Bread-face tugged him closer.

"Today's ritual will be simple," Temple Keeper said. "You have a wandering ghost who is all alone, with no family shrine to call its home. It is a common ghost. I can easily remove it from your hall."

"If they're so common, why are they lonely? Why don't they make friends with each other?" Jack asked.

"Hush!" Old Bread-face whispered. "This is no time for silly questions."

"Not silly at all," Temple Keeper remarked. "The strongest human connections are family ties, and even ghosts need them. But wandering ghosts were unexpectedly cut off from their loved ones in the living world. They're doomed to drift alone until they make a connection with a companion or their family. The world of the dead is not like a public market, where spirits gather and trade gossip."

Jack and Old Bread-face watched from one side as Temple Keeper set up an altar table. He lit two candles and placed them next to an oil lamp set in a fancy brass base. Then he poured tea into one bowl and water into another, placing one on each side of a dish of cooked rice. He set out five plates, each holding fresh fruit. He lit incense sticks and set them in a jar at the centre of the altar. As their fragrance filled the room, Temple Keeper leaned an eight-sided mirror against the jar and chanted softly. "*Nah-mo-aw-lay-toh-fat! Nah-mo-aw-lay-toh-fat!*"

If I can learn these chants, then maybe I can use them to chase away ghosts.

"Watch the incense sticks as they burn," Old Bread-face whispered to Jack. "The smoke ascends to heaven while the ashes drop down to the earth. That is similar to what happens when someone dies and the soul leaves its body behind."

I hope the ghost vanishes along with the incense smoke.

Temple Keeper slowly circled the table, swinging a little bell high and then low. He placed handfuls of uncooked rice in four spots on the floor, marking a square around the altar. Then he picked up a short stubby sword. It had no sharp edges because it was made from Chinese coins laced firmly together with red string. All the while, he kept chanting in a low steady voice.

"This sword is very powerful," Old Bread-face whispered. "The coins are made from the five earthly elements: air, fire, wood, water and metal. The sword unifies the power of all the elements to drive away evil. If you know how to wield this sword, then you can defeat ghosts."

Jack nodded.

Next, Temple Keeper reached into a wicker basket and pulled out a live chicken. The fat brown creature gave a startled squawk and then fell silent. Temple Keeper strode back and forth in front of the altar. His arms moved in small circles, offering the plump bird to the spirit world. Then he tucked it under one arm, pulled out a sharp penknife and slit its throat. The chicken jerked and tried to flap its wings, but Temple Keeper held it firmly, letting the blood gush into a large empty pot.

Gently placing the dead chicken on the floor, Temple Keeper picked up a writing brush, dipped it into the blood and mixed the blood with some black ink. Next he used the bloody ink to write words on sheets of yellow paper and on squares of white cloth. With a dab of glue, he fastened both paper and cloth to the front side of the table. Then he rang the bell, chanting loudly and softly, loudly and softly. He held up an earthenware jar and moved it around in circles before slamming a metal cap over the jar's mouth.

"He just trapped the ghost in the jar," Old Bread-face exclaimed. "The ritual is over!" He hurried over to offer congratulations.

"I must get the jar and the chicken to the temple right away," Temple Keeper said. "Old Bread-face, you carry the oil lamp, but be careful that the flame does not go out."

"All right."

Temple Keeper turned to Jack and said, "The altar and all

the sacred objects must be left in place overnight. Wait until the candles burn out before you go. No matter what happens, don't leave before then. Oh, and here's the anti-ghost charm for Yu-yi."

After the two men left, Jack cautiously walked around the altar. He glanced at the little piles of rice grain. They would have to be swept up before they attracted mice. He studied the wall charms that Temple Keeper had written with chicken blood. He had no idea what the words meant. Then he picked up the magic sword and hefted its weight. The coins glittered in the dim candlelight. Jack thrust it forward just as Temple Keeper had done.

"*Nah-mo-aw-lay-toh-fat!*" he chanted.

Suddenly a ghost appeared at the tip of the sword—the same young woman as before. Jack stepped back and gasped.

She wore the same blue Chinese smock, but this time Jack saw that its edges were decorated with shiny bands of black material. Her hair neatly framed her face, and a bun coiled behind her head. She had a pretty face, a small mouth and a pockmark on her cheekbone just under the left edge of her right eye.

Then she was gone.

Temple Keeper failed! We wasted our money. All his efforts were worthless. That ghost is more powerful than Temple Keeper. We can't reopen the nickelodeon yet!

There was a sudden knocking behind him. As he whirled around, the front door shot open and the bright sunlight blinded him for a moment.

"Bad news," Kern cried out. Then his mouth dropped open. "What's going on?"

Jack almost blurted out that the ritual had failed, but he caught himself. "Temple Keeper came to drive away the ghost."

There could be big trouble if news leaked out that the ghost was still here.

"I hope he got rid of it," Kern said, walking over to the altar. He looked around but didn't touch anything. One hand fingered a little brocade case hanging from a cord around his neck.

"He caught it in a jar and took it to the temple," Jack said. "He told me to stay until the last candle burns out."

"Father is sending me to China next week," Kern blurted out. "Ma already bought my ticket. I saw it. I'm sailing on the *Manchuria*."

Oh no! That's the end of my free meals at the noodle house!

"They want me to get a Chinese education, so they're sending me to Uncle Wing."

At least Kern won't be around to pester me to help steal money.

"But I'm not going," Kern said.

"What? What will you do—run away?"

"That's exactly it! I'll get a job on a farm, maybe in Marysville. They always need workers. I'm strong enough."

"Hey, dummy, the harvest is already over."

"Don't call me dummy!"

"You won't find work. You'll starve to death."

"I just need enough money to get me through the winter. I've thought this through. I'll be fine as soon as spring planting starts. But you've got to help me get more money. I don't have enough."

"Is that why you keep scheming to steal from people?"

"Father had mentioned China a few times, but I never thought he was serious!"

"But your mother is always saying that life here is better than there. She doesn't really want you to go there, does she?"

"She does. In fact I'm sure it was her idea."

The candles finally sputtered out, and the boys left the hall. Jack padlocked the front door. *No thief would dare break into a haunted building.*

"So you'll help me get some cash?" Kern asked, as they walked away.

"Maybe, if you have a good plan."

"I do. Tonight, when you go to the opium den, steal money from a dozing customer. It'll be easy!"

"That's your plan? I steal the money and hand it to you? That's not fair. What if I get caught? What if a customer calls the police? They're always looking for an excuse to raid your father's place."

"Don't worry! The smokers lie there in dreamland for hours. Then they stagger out and go home in a daze. They won't remember how much money they had."

"But it's my first day on the job!"

They heard the clatter of horses' hooves galloping over the cobblestones. A fire bell clanged louder and louder.

"Fire!" Kern shouted.

Both boys ran down the street, turned a corner and saw the gleaming pumper pull up in front of the Wing Fung Garment Factory.

Dark smoke billowed out of the third-floor windows. The firemen barked out instructions, connected the hoses and dragged them inside. Onlookers spilled out of surrounding buildings onto the street, blocking wagons and automobiles. The boys elbowed their way to the front, eager to see some action. They were soon disappointed because the blaze turned out not to be serious at all. In no time, the firemen extinguished it. As they began rolling up and packing up their equipment, Jack saw Yu-yi.

He ran to her and asked, "Are you all right?"

She nodded, but her eyes were large with fear.

"How did the fire start?"

"I was stacking boxes in the front when an oil lamp suddenly fell." She stammered as she spoke. "It landed on a pile of cloth scraps and started burning."

"It was an accident?"

Yu-yi hesitated before answering. "I think Lincoln made it happen because he wants me to join him in the ghost world."

"Lincoln wouldn't do that!" Jack protested.

"But I saw him in the mirror last night again." Her face crumpled as if she was about to weep. She pressed a knuckle to her lip to stop the trembling. "And he kept waving at me to join him, just like before."

Jack glanced around to make sure no one was watching and said, "Show me the mirror, while everyone is still outside."

Yu-yi led him to the back entrance. The air was heavy with the smell of smoke. They hurried upstairs to a tiny room on the top floor.

Yu-yi opened the door and pointed. "That's the mirror where I saw him."

Jack looked. "I don't see anything. Do you?"

"Not now. But he was there last night."

"Here, take this." Jack pulled out the charm from Temple Keeper. "It's an anti-ghost charm to protect you."

Yu-yi clutched it tightly to her heart and took a deep gulp of air. Then she smiled at Jack.

They heard footsteps downstairs. As Yu-yi turned toward the door, Jack saw the ghost girl again. She was staring at him in the mirror. Her hair was tied up in a bun. He noticed the pockmark under her left eye. She seemed to be just a couple of years older than him. A chill went up his back. *What is she doing here? Is she following me?* She stayed only a moment, then faded away. This was the closest she had come to him, and now he was sure he had never met her before.

"Hurry. We have to leave. Someone's coming," Yu-yi whispered.

CHAPTER FIVE

Tuesday, Early Evening

J ack whistled a cheerful tune, trying to look nonchalant. He was on his way to Cat Uncle's shop, with his hands inside his trouser pockets. He kicked a stone over the sidewalk. He was getting close to Broadway, and made sure not to cross it because Kern had warned him that white boys would hurl rocks at him if he did. Chinatown residents had come home with serious injuries from such attacks, so Jack also avoided crossing Chinatown's other border streets: Powell, Kearny and California.

Jack couldn't stop thinking about Yu-yi. Such a pretty smile. He could see why Lincoln had been soft on her. Once or twice he looked around to see if Lincoln might be following him. Mostly he saw construction men leaving worksites.

Cat King's opium shop was run out of a storefront located

far from the centre of Chinatown where it would not offend the Chinese community. Also, white customers could safely approach it without being seen. The building looked like a long box and was made from low-grade lumber. Jack had seen livestock barns around Marysville that were better built and in better condition.

As Jack sauntered to the door, Guard Uncle was placing long boards in front of the plate glass windows to protect them overnight.

"Hey, Guard Uncle," he called politely.

"Hey, boy," he grunted back. "You're late."

"There was a fire."

"I heard the fire wagons. Where was it?"

"Wing Fung. It was a small blaze. Nothing to see."

Guard Uncle rapped three times on the heavy door. "That's the knock you use when you want to get in," he said. "Go through the curtain at the back. Your Cat Uncle is waiting for you."

An eye peered through a peephole. Then someone released an iron bolt and opened the door. Jack slipped inside and walked past a big glass case overflowing with tobacco tins, slim wooden boxes of cigars, British-style pipes, all types of Chinese incense and a large variety of candies and chocolates. Atop the counter lay the day's newspapers and lottery tickets and a teapot. A brass pendulum swung under a wall clock next to a sign reading CASH ONLY in both English and Chinese. In the corner stood two high-back chairs for customers to sit on and pass the time. The place looked like any other tobacco shop.

As Jack stepped behind the curtain, he was engulfed by heavy smoke. The backroom was larger than the shop, but there was no electricity, only gas lamps. In the dim light Jack saw several men lying on cots, smoking long pipes. Some had removed their shoes to get more comfortable, while others kept their boots on. Cat King stood to one side, welcoming an old Chinese labourer, sweaty and grubby from the day's work, and two white customers wearing business suits and ties.

After settling his clients with lamps and pillows, Cat Uncle led Jack to a square table holding a tray of restaurant food and a rack of tiny opium bowls. The light was so weak that Jack had to lean close to see clearly.

All that was left were discarded chicken bones, one big bowl of rice and a dish of vegetables with bean curd.

They must have just finished dinner. I should have come earlier!

"Eat your fill, then clear the table and scrape out the opium bowls," Cat King ordered, pushing the rack toward Jack.

Cat King started rolling little balls of opium paste. "I want you to treat my customers with respect. Some of these old men have lived here for fifty years, ever since the gold rush. They haven't seen their wives or children who still live in China."

"Why don't their families come here?"

"The US laws say they cannot. So the men are all alone. No money to send back either."

"What should I do after I clean the bowls?"

"Make sure the lamps have enough oil. Good thing you speak both English and Chinese. Everyone will be wondering who you are. Tell the customers you are my new helper. They all worry about informers and police raids."

Jack's chopsticks clattered in the bowl. As he wolfed down the food, he gazed at the dozing customers. Some had their eyes wide open, their pupils catching the light of the flames, glittering softly in the dark, like stars. Other men's eyes were closed, and their breathing was steady and even.

I can't steal their money. Maybe I should tell Cat Uncle that Kern is going to run away.

But Jack was too scared to say anything. He was so hungry that he didn't leave a single grain of rice in his bowl. "Shall I take the dishes back to the restaurant now?"

"What if you drop them? Who will pay for them? A waiter will take them later when we send out for snacks."

Jack carefully scraped out the opium bowls and wiped them clean with a cloth. Then he lugged a can of oil to fill the lamps. But when he filled the oil lamps, each man jolted awake and grunted, asking who he was and what he wanted.

"I'm Cat King's new helper," Jack said, all the while looking for someone who had loosened his grip on his pipe or someone whose head sagged limply on the pillow.

Maybe I can get away with stealing some money for Kern. He shouldn't be sent off to China. He'll hate it there!

The man in the second-to-last cot seemed to be fast asleep, and Jack eyed his pockets. The flaps did not have buttons. He knelt beside the man and nudged him. He didn't stir. Jack's hand shook as he poured oil into the lamp next to the man. He glanced behind him to see if Cat King was watching. He wasn't, but when Jack turned back, he almost screamed.

His brother was perched on the edge of the man's cot, staring intently at Jack. He was wearing the same shirt from the day of the earthquake.

Someone grabbed Jack's shoulder. He jumped and yelped, almost knocking over the oil can.

"Is something wrong?" Cat Uncle asked. "You look as if you saw a ghost. Get the broom and sweep the floor."

There was a loud banging at the front of the store. As it grew more forceful, Guard Uncle and the doorman rushed in. "It's the police!" Guard Uncle shouted. "They're using axes to chop down the front door!"

Some customers rushed to the back door. Others continued to dream, lying on their cots.

"Open the windows!" a customer shouted. "Let us out!"

"They've surrounded us," Cat King declared. "There's no escape!"

Jack ran to a window, but it was covered with wooden planks that were nailed tight to prevent the telltale smoke from leaking out.

I'm going to get caught and land in jail and then Ma is going to kill me!

The sound of splintering wood came from the back door.

"Don't you have an escape plan?" the man in the business suit yelled. "How can you run a place like this without having one?"

"No need worry," Cat King said in English. He patted the customer's back to calm him. "Police take you downtown, but no book white man. You no spend night in jail."

Then he turned to the other customers and spoke in Chinese. "Everyone, listen! There's nothing to fear from the police. Tomorrow when you go before the judge, plead guilty and pay the fine. Then come here and I'll give you your money back."

The customers moaned about their bad luck.

"A night in jail!" someone snapped.

"We'll get beat up," another muttered.

"Your front-door guard should have warned us. He must have been asleep," someone yelled.

"Didn't you pay off the police to stay away?" another asked.

Jack's entire body shook with fear.

Help me, someone!

He saw Lincoln's ghost gesturing for him to follow. Jack hesitated for only half a second. His brother led the way to a little storage room and pointed to two boards in the floor. In the faint light, Jack groped frantically at their edges. Then he lifted them, jumped down and landed with a crunch on the gravel foundation below. Just as he replaced the boards above him and lay down, he heard a crash and cheers from the police who had broken through the back door.

"Throw them all in the paddy wagons!"

"Hurry! They're running away!"

I'm safe! Jack thought.

"Give me a crowbar," a voice shouted. "They'll run to their secret tunnels. They dug them everywhere under Chinatown."

Jack held his breath as he heard someone prying up the nearby floorboards. Meanwhile, the sharp edges of broken brick and rubble dug into his back.

Slowly the clamour above him died down. Everyone must have been arrested. Then he heard the planks squeaking over his head as footsteps probed the boards.

"Hey, something looks fishy here!"

More footsteps. Then a bright light shone through the cracks in the boards above him. A boot nudged the planks. Jack wanted to crawl away as fast as he could, but he dared not move, fearing that he might get lost in the darkness.

Suddenly Jack heard a loud rattling.

"What the devil is that!"

Jack heard a soft thud followed by rapid footsteps.

"Get out of here, quick!"

Jack lay still until all the sounds of the police had faded away.

Something scurried by him, brushing his cheek. A rat! Were more coming? Jack covered his head with his arms.

Finally Jack couldn't stand it anymore. He sat up and raised the boards, slowly and silently in case an officer had stayed behind. Then he slipped through the back door and darted away down the dark streets.

He opened the apartment door, hoping that Ma would be asleep, but she was waiting for him. She looked worried. "Did you give Yu-yi the anti-ghost charm from Temple Keeper?" she demanded.

"Yes, I saw her right after the fire."

"She's all right?"

Jack nodded.

Ma sighed with relief and said, "A careless worker knocked over an oil lamp. Cat Aunty told me all about it. Luckily there wasn't too much damage. But the smoke fumes will make the Wing Fung shipments stink."

That's not the way Yu-yi told it!

Jack took a deep breath and asked the question that had bothered him all afternoon. "Ma, now that Yu-yi is protected, will Lincoln look for other girls to be his ghost bride?"

"He would never do that," Ma declared. "The only reason

your brother went after Yu-yi was to save her from Old Kong."
She glanced at her watch. "Where have you been?" she asked.
"Why weren't you home earlier?"

"I was with Kern."

"Liar! Kern came here looking for you. How did you get so
dirty?"

"George and Albert were chasing me, and I had to hide in
a shed."

"Your brother would never lie to me like that." Ma turned
away and sank onto a chair. "If only your father were here! He
would beat you for lying. Now go clean up and get to bed."

"Where's your medicine?"

"There's no more."

"I'll get some, Ma. You need to get better."

"If you want that, then stop telling lies."

Jack reddened and turned away.

"What about the ghost in the nickelodeon? Did Temple
Keeper get rid of it?"

"Yes."

She'll feel better if she thinks the ghost is gone.

"Was it Lincoln?" she asked.

"Temple Keeper said it was a female."

"How could that be?" Ma frowned. "We lived in that
building for half a year and never saw anything strange."

Jack shrugged and hurried away.

Minutes later he huddled under his blankets trying to fall
asleep. But the image of Lincoln's ghost and the ghost from the
nickelodeon, and the thud of the police boots, kept spinning
around in his head.

CHAPTER SIX

Wednesday Morning

J ack slept badly. His arms and legs ached. All night he was plagued by bad dreams—nightmares that felt so real and bothersome that he was relieved to wake up. As he stumbled into the kitchen, Anna and Constance tugged at him to play chase with them. He almost lost his temper and scolded them.

"Can't you let them go and run around outside, like Lincoln and I used to do on the farm?" Jack asked Ma.

"It's not safe," Ma snapped. "There aren't enough Chinese women here. You want criminals to steal the girls and sell them?"

I wish I could skip school and sleep all day, but Ma would never allow it.

Ma was stir-frying leftover rice, chopped green onions and

eggs in a hot wok. They sizzled, and a delicious smell filled the kitchen.

There was a knock at the door and Anna ran to open it.

Guard Uncle limped into the kitchen as Jack set down his bowl. "Boy, are you all right?"

"What are you talking about?" Ma asked, wiping her hands on her apron and greeting him.

Behind her back, Jack waved frantically at Guard Uncle and put a warning finger to his lips.

"The fire . . ." Guard Uncle stuttered as his gaze darted from Ma to Jack and then back to Ma. He paused and yanked his hat off his head. "Uh . . . after the fire wagons left, I saw Jack running along Dupont Street. He tripped and it looked like he hurt himself. He got up and walked like me—one leg straight, one leg crooked."

"That was when I was being chased by George and Albert," Jack added.

Ma gave Jack a cold stare.

"Would you like some rice?" she asked their visitor.

"No, thank you. You are kind to ask." He threw Jack a questioning glance. "Glad to see you are fine."

Then the doorman hurried away.

Ma grabbed the feather duster and whacked the bamboo handle on the table. Jack winced at the loud crack.

"You're working for Cat Uncle, aren't you?" Ma said.

"It's to help us pay the rent."

"I don't care. You can't work for him! I don't want you smoking opium."

"I wouldn't ever do that, and you know it. I'm not stupid."

"I don't want you landing in prison!"

"Cat Uncle didn't let me get arrested last night, even though everyone else got taken to jail."

"The police raided Cat Uncle's shop?" Ma's eyes widened.

"But nothing happened to me! See? I'm safe and sound!"

"Your uncle is a criminal." She turned away angrily.

"Don't treat me like a baby, Ma," Jack protested. "We have to get money. Old Kong threatened to evict us! You want us to live on the street? We'll freeze to death!"

"I'll deal with Old Kong. Next time he comes by, tell him to talk to me. I know how to take care of things."

Ma flung her apron off, stormed out of the kitchen and slammed the door to her room.

Jack got to school just as Mrs. Newhall stopped swinging the bell. He rushed to his seat. Miss Strickland had not arrived yet.

"Dungeon-boy, dungeon-boy," his classmates started to chant. "Eat chicken poop, and dead bok choy. *Gahm-dun doi, gahm-dun doi, hek gai see, hek lahn choi.*"

The taunting grew louder. Shrieking with laughter, everyone banged the tables and stomped their feet in time with the rhyme. A spitball hit Jack's forehead. Jack clenched his fists tightly under the desk.

When the teacher finally came in, the racket immediately subsided. After the class stumbled through singing "Hail, Columbia," Miss Strickland called the roll. First period was silent reading, so Jack opened his textbook to the poem *The Highwayman*. It was about ghosts haunting an old English inn and reminded Jack about Yu-yi and Lincoln's ghost.

Lincoln misses her. He must be lonely in the ghost world.

Time dragged on like a plough behind a lame horse. In the afternoon there was penmanship—the class that Jack hated the most. To draw every stroke the perfect shape and the right thickness took too much concentration, and Ma always complained about having to scrub the ink off his cuff.

At the end of the school day, Kern was waiting in the schoolyard. Jack smiled when he saw George and Albert keeping a safe distance away.

"Want something to eat?" Kern asked. "I saw a fresh tray of cakes at the Far East."

"Shouldn't you be saving your money?"

Kern ignored him. "Hey, did you hear what Old Fong said? If you walk in and leave without buying any cakes, then you should still pay him something for inhaling the sweet aromas."

Jack didn't laugh, and asked instead, "Did you hear what I said about saving money?"

The boys started walking down the hill. New buildings stood straight and tall among the wreckage in Chinatown and the business district, while the bright blue of the sky and the bay seemed to promise better times for all.

"Cakes are cheap," Kern said, throwing an arm over Jack's shoulder and drawing him close. "As for getting money, I have a new idea."

"Don't give me any trouble." Jack shoved him away. "I just missed spending a night in jail."

"Guard Uncle told me. How did you get away?"

"I hid under the floorboards."

"You're lucky the police didn't grab you. They always poke around for secret tunnels. Don't they know there aren't any?"

"I thought I was doomed!"

"The shop is closed for a while. You'll need to get money for the rent."

"So?"

"So why won't you help me with my new scheme?"

"Because I don't want to get caught!"

"What about me! I could die in China! You know people die there easily. Remember the second son of Wing Hing Lung? He died just four months after arriving in China! People get sick and die there all the time. A single insect bite will kill you. The doctors have no cures."

"Things are bad here too! The jail is dirty and dank. The drinking water is filthy. The guards could shoot me dead and no one would ever know."

"You won't get caught! I promise!"

"Your promises never work out."

"But I've got the best plan ever! Just hear me out!"

The cousins glared at each other. Finally Jack said, "All right. What is it?"

Kern lowered his voice and said, "I can get us into any room in our apartment building. Old Kong left a copy of the master key with Ba in case of an emergency. I know where Ba hid it. I'll sneak in to someone's room and steal money. All you have to do is stand guard."

"Hey, Jack!" William Uncle came running across the road.

"Meet me at my place later this evening," Kern whispered, before slipping away.

"Are you showing films yet?" William Uncle asked. "I need to play the piano as often as I can. It keeps my fingers loose and nimble." He wiggled them in the air for Jack to see.

"Old Bread-face hasn't said anything," Jack replied. "I need to go to his store and ask."

A waiter from a nearby restaurant ran by them with a covered tray of rattling dishes. He was delivering hot food to one of the stores. As he passed a group of men, someone stuck out a foot. The waiter tripped and his tray fell with a crash. Everyone laughed and shouted "Clumsy!" and "No eyes!" at him. Luckily, Chinatown's stray dogs raced up and gobbled the food, so the angry waiter only had to sweep up the broken dishes. He seemed too scared to pick a fight.

"Old Bread-face is a fool," William Uncle said. "He believes everything that Temple Keeper says. There are no such things as ghosts. We should have reopened right away instead of delaying. Temple Keeper is just looking for ways to make money."

Jack nodded politely. William Uncle was a Christian, which was why most of the men in Chinatown didn't talk to him. Christians believed that their Almighty God protected them from evil. When people died, their souls either went to heaven or hell. They never came back as ghosts, because hell was a well-guarded cave deep underground, and who would ever want to leave paradise?

Jack knew this from attending church in Marysville, but he had stopped going after he saw ghosts there. One Sunday he had seen old Mr. Sullivan, the husband of the choir leader, standing right beside the minister and singing happily even though Mr. Sullivan's funeral had happened just a week before. Nevertheless, Lincoln went regularly on Sundays, thinking he could learn new things there or make new friends.

"I know! I'll ask my minister to conduct a service in the hall," said William Uncle. "We will sing hymns and pray to God. That'll fix things."

Jack could see the bell tower of Saint Mary's Cathedral. The Chinese called it the Big Clock Building. The bell tower and church walls had miraculously survived the great fire, even though the flames had been so hot that the church's great bell had melted. The charred walls were still standing when the Leongs had moved back to Chinatown. So there might be something to William Uncle's faith.

"Go talk to Old Bread-face about doing that," Jack suggested. "Sounds like a good idea."

"He never listens to me."

"He never listens to me either."

They both laughed.

"Go ask Old Bread-face when the next show is," he said, waving goodbye to Jack.

Outside Old Bread-face's general store, Sing Chong Company, workers unloaded a shipment from China, heaving wooden crates and huge earthenware jars off a horse-drawn wagon. The two horses stood patiently, flicking their tails at flies. Inside, the smell of fresh rice and salted fish and preserved meats filled the air. Sawdust had been spread on the floor to absorb any spillage from the pans of pickled vegetables, bean sprouts and tofu.

Old Chang, the head clerk, smiled broadly, showing a mouthful of gold teeth. "Hey, Jackson," he called. "Long time no see. How come?"

He tossed over three coconut candies. Each was wrapped in lightweight rice paper that melted in your mouth. Jack caught them deftly. "School. Homework. Babysitting."

"Ah, you're getting too smart for old men like us. The boss is in his office."

As Jack opened the door, Old Bread-face was beaming. "Jackson, good news!"

"We're reopening?"

"Sunday. It is the white man's holy day. Maybe that will bring us good luck. The new films are here, so we will get a good crowd. There's time to make posters. You can go around and put them up tomorrow after school."

"Can't you get one of your clerks to do it?"

Old Bread-face went on. "I received word from the Chinese consulate that the consul will attend our reopening. Isn't that wonderful! It will be announced in the Chinese newspapers, and all the big shots in Chinatown will want to attend. We need to clean up the place and make sure we have enough seats."

That doesn't leave much time to get rid of the ghost.

"Jackson, why are you frowning? This is the best publicity of all. Check the projector. Make sure it runs perfectly. Do we need to buy oil?"

"No." Jack thought for a moment before asking, "When you and Temple Keeper went back to the temple, did he tell you anything about the ghost?"

"Hush!" Old Bread-face rushed to close the office door and said, "When people hear that word, they think you are inviting evil spirits in."

"What did Temple Keeper tell you about the ghost?"

"Nothing."

"Did you ever hear about a ghost in the outhouse behind the nickelodeon?"

"Everybody has heard about it, but nobody has ever seen it. Why do you ask?"

"I just want to make sure nothing disturbs our reopening."

"Oh, by the way, tell your mother this. Don't do any piecework for Wing Fung. Old Fung went to the temple to get ghost charms. He thinks his new building might have a ghost."

Jack swallowed hard. *It's Lincoln's ghost. And the ghost girl was there too.*

"On your way home, go to Chun Wo Tong," Old Bread-face said. "This morning Old Yao talked to me. He noticed your mother stopped buying her medicine. He suspects she doesn't have the money. But her health won't improve unless she drinks the herbal tea. So pick it up on your way home, and make sure she brews it. Tell Old Yao to put it on my account."

"Ma dislikes the medicine," Jack reminded him. "She says when she drinks it, her heart beats faster, her hands start to tremble and she gets nightmares."

"Ah, she just wants to avoid the bitter taste."

"Not true! Ma knows that only bitter teas can heal a person. She says the more awful the tea tastes, the faster it will work."

But Old Bread-face had already turned away.

At Chun Wo Tong, the herbalist was hunched over a prescription. He looked two hundred years old, with white whiskers and thick spectacles. Old Yao received Jack politely and shuffled off to measure the dried plants, seeds, nuts and animal parts that had been prescribed for Ma's liver. Jack watched him weigh the ingredients, planning to ask him about Gee Uncle's outhouse ghost story. But when Old Yao handed him the packets and reminded him how to brew the tea, Jack didn't say a word.

No one in Chinatown will tell me anything. People are too afraid of ghosts.

When Jack got home, Old Kong the landlord was waiting for him.

"Well, well, well," he drawled. "I see you have money to buy expensive medicine."

"Old Bread-face paid for this. You don't want Ma to die, do you?"

"Where's the rent money?" He spat a toothpick onto the street. "Do you want your family sleeping on the street?"

"Sunday night, after the show. That's when you'll get it."

CHAPTER SEVEN

Wednesday Evening

Cat Uncle's family lived in one of the large apartments that faced the street. Sunshine streamed in through the front windows, and Cat Aunty's racks of plants and flowers flourished. Kern had helped his father build the shelves, making sure they were sturdy enough for the heavy pots.

Kern greeted Jack at the door. "The old ones aren't home. They went to a Founder's Day banquet for the Louie clan. They'll be late, so we'll have plenty of time to sneak into some apartments."

"I don't think this is a good idea."

In response Kern held out the steamship ticket.

"It's for Sunday, the same day that the nickelodeon reopens. There isn't much time to get the money we need."

Jack flipped over the ticket and saw that the back was stamped with the words: NO REFUND. ALL SALES FINAL. Jack sighed and felt sorry for his cousin. Cat Aunty and Uncle weren't joking about the trip to China.

He walked into the sitting room, which he always imagined to be exactly the same as a white American home. It was much better furnished than his apartment. Here, the Western-style chairs had soft springy seats and wide armrests. Lamps with fringed shades sat on side tables with curved legs. A phonograph with a gleaming horn dominated a music cabinet made of polished wood. In the middle of the room was a trunk bound with gleaming metal strips. It looked as if it weighed a ton.

"I've seen bigger ones," Jack said, "two or three times as high."

"Oh, but this one fits under my bed on the ship," Kern said, imitating his mother's shrill tone and kicking the trunk. The thump made one of Cat Aunty's cats run away. "It has a sheet-iron bottom, brass corners and rubber bumpers."

The Siamese lay purring on the rug. Its intense green eyes burned bright as jewels. Jack bent down and ran his hand through its fur and it purred contentedly.

"That's the expert hunter, " Kern said. "She'll track down a mouse, trap it in a corner and play with it for half an hour. Then she grabs it by the neck and kills it."

"Our farm had cats. Some of them brought back dead birds in their mouths."

"I wish Old Kong would let us keep dogs in this building. Guard animals are more useful than these cats."

On the wall were faded yellow squares of cloth and paper

covered with Chinese brushwork. Jack leaned forward and looked at them closely. *They're exactly like the ones that Temple Keeper wrote in blood ink at the nickelodeon.*

Kern called from the kitchen. "Eat something," he said, pointing to the chopping block on the counter. A long slab of barbecued pork had been cut into thick slices. The succulent meat glistened with sauce.

"Is that your dinner?"

Kern shrugged. "Mother asked me what I wanted for dinner, and this is what I told her. She's feeling guilty about sending me to China."

"What's the plan for tonight?" Jack asked.

"We wait for someone rich like Ping Chong to go gambling for the night and sneak into his place."

"That won't work. He lives just two doors away from me."

"But we could get a lot of money from his place."

"But he'll suspect me. He knows that Ma is sick and that we need money for the rent and medicine."

"Let's go knock on doors on the third floor and see who isn't at home."

"How about we stand by your door and see who goes out first?"

"Because our door would be open and that person might catch us watching. Then *we'd* get blamed."

"Don't you know which tenants have already gone out?"

"How would I know that?"

"You've been home for hours."

"I don't stand at the door and watch people go in and out."

"So what do you do all day?"

"What does it matter? Let's just go upstairs and knock on

doors. If someone answers, then I'll say the power went off in our apartment and I was wondering if their power was out too."

Jack shook his head. "Listen, after you steal the money, someone will remember that you came to their door with that stupid question."

"It's not a stupid question!"

"If the power died in here, then you would go next door, not upstairs!"

"You really don't want to help, do you?"

Jack shrugged.

"Then how will you get the rent money?"

"From customers. When the nickelodeon reopens on Sunday. Guess what? The Chinese consul will be coming, so there'll be a big crowd."

"Not if that ghost comes back."

"It won't come back! I'll make sure of it!"

"Don't be such a coward! Let's get the key," Kern said. Jack hung back before following him into the master bedroom. On the wall was a Chinese landscape painting, a calendar from the *China West Daily* newspaper and a two-line poem brushed in big words on long scrolls. The Western-style bed had metal posts, little angels flying along the headboard, and electric lamps mounted over the pillows. A bright-red quilt featured a giant version of the Chinese word for "joyous marriage." Kern went to a wooden chest and lifted the cover. The strong smell of cedar rushed out.

"Should we open the window?" Jack asked. "What if your parents come home and smell the wood and figure out you opened the chest?"

"Will you shut up?" Kern lifted the top tray from the chest, set it aside and removed piles of folded clothes. He stacked everything in neat rows.

Jack put his hands behind his back, not wanting to touch anything. The tray was filled with old photographs, each mounted in a stiff cardboard frame. He moved closer to get a better look, and what he saw sent a chill up his back.

The ghost girl!

Cat Uncle, Cat Aunty and the ghost girl were standing in front of a Chinatown store. She had a pretty face, a small mouth and a pockmark on her cheekbone just under the left edge of her right eye. Kern's parents looked young and happy. Jack turned over the photograph. The studio's name was stamped on the back, along with the date, AUGUST 1893.

Then Jack noticed the address over the door—840. It was the same building that was now the nickelodeon.

"Do you know this girl?" Jack asked.

"That's Mei, my mother's servant."

"Where is she now?"

"Don't know. Ma said she ran away to the Chinese Mission."

"That place burned down after the earthquake, didn't it?"

"Don't know. Here's the key. Put the picture back. Let's go!"

"You do it."

Kern yanked the photograph from Jack and slipped it into the chest.

"Yahhh!" a woman screamed. The shrill sound came from inside the building.

Is it Ma? Jack wondered.

Then he heard the same voice scream again, louder.

"It's Ma!" he cried out.

As the boys raced into the hallway, Old Hoy opened his door, wearing his pyjamas. "What's all this screaming?" he demanded. "Jack, is your mother crazy?"

The door to Jack's apartment was wide open. Ma stood there panting. Jack's sisters clutched at her apron. The smell of Ma's herbal medicine lingered in the air.

Jack rushed to her. "What's wrong , Ma? Are you sick?"

He tried to coax Ma back into the apartment, but her eyes were wide with fear.

"I'm not going back in there!"

Jack waved at Kern to step back. "You'd better go. I'll handle this." He put an arm around Ma, led her back in and closed the door.

"Everything will be okay," he said. "No need to be afraid. Come on, sit down."

"Don't go into your room. I saw a ghost there!"

So, Ma has yin-yang eyes too!

"Was it Lincoln?" he asked.

"No." Ma shuddered. "Jack, you were right about that. I was foolish to think Lincoln was angry with me."

Anna and Constance were sobbing from fear. Jack went to them, but didn't know what to do. Then he remembered Old Chang's gifts from that afternoon. He rifled through his pocket and handed each girl a candy. "Anna, take Constance to your room and play with the flower cards."

After they left, Jack led Ma into the kitchen. Her hands were as cold as ice. She sagged in her chair and closed her eyes. Her face was deathly pale. Jack had never seen her look so haggard.

He filled the kettle and put it on the stove for tea. "What

happened, Ma?" he asked softly.

"I went into your room to pull the blind," she said. "I passed by the mirror. I looked in it and saw a woman standing beside me. 'Go away!' I shouted at her, and she vanished."

"What did she look like?"

"I couldn't see the face clearly, but it was a young woman. Her hair was in a bun. She was wearing blue."

It's the ghost from the nickelodeon! She's everywhere!

CHAPTER EIGHT

Thursday Morning

"**C**razy Lady! Crazy Lady!" Albert shouted, leaping from one desk to another. *"Sun ging deen-paw! Sun ging deen-paw!"*

"Crazy Lady! Crazy Lady!" The rest of the class joined the ruckus. But they all kept an eye on the door, because Miss Strickland could return at any moment.

Jack ignored the taunt and opened his textbook to the Declaration of Independence.

"Crazy Lady! Crazy Lady!" Albert shouted in Jack's ear.

Then Jack leaped up and dashed to Miss Strickland's desk. Nobody was allowed to touch anything on the teacher's table, ever. But he grabbed her long ruler and slammed it down as hard as he could. The gunshot crack silenced everyone.

Jack ran over and swung the ruler at Albert's head. "You want me to hit you?" he shouted.

"No!" Albert raised one hand to protect his skull.

George tried to push his way in, but Jack spun around and jabbed the ruler into his chest. "Sit!" he shouted. "Or I'll crack your head."

George obeyed, and Jack turned back to Albert. "You want me to insult your mother?"

"No."

"Then why are you making fun of mine?"

Albert stared straight ahead.

"Albert, is there something you want to tell the class about my mother?" asked Jack.

"No."

"Then keep your mouth shut." Jack turned and tossed the ruler back onto Miss Strickland's desk. Just as he sat down, the door flew open and she walked in.

Jack's hands trembled. He was flabbergasted. Never before had he imagined daring to take on Albert and George by himself.

They'll stay away from me now.

Jack frowned, deep in thought. He wondered which of his classmates' servants might have known Cat Aunty's servant girl Mei. Alice Lam's nanny, Old Four, was by far the oldest of his classmates' servants. She had a grim dark face and snarled at anyone who had the back luck to stumble against her. Alice always scolded Old Four for forgetting things, so maybe her memory wasn't the best. Charlotte Fong's man was a few years younger than Old Four, but he was completely deaf.

"Jackson Leong!" Miss Strickland's voice shattered his calm. "Stand up!"

His face reddened as every face in the classroom swivelled around at him.

"Did you hear the question I asked you?"

"No, Ma'am."

"Why not?"

"I wasn't listening. I was daydreaming. I won't do it again."

His classmates tittered and turned to Miss Strickland, eager to see how she would punish him.

"Go stand in the corner until lunchtime, Jackson!"

At the end of the day, Miss Strickland kept him in for fifteen minutes, so it was too late for him to talk to any servants.

After school Jack hurried to the nickelodeon. A stack of handbills that Old Bread-face had printed lay by the door. Jack groaned. Then he grabbed them along with a pot of glue and a brush and went off to put them up.

A year and a half after the earthquake, Chinatown was just a fraction of the crowded neighbourhood it once had been. All the construction sites were surrounded by tall fences to keep out thieves and squatters. These barricades were already plastered with posters and handbills announcing various events and products. Jack's handbills from two weeks ago, announcing the grand opening of the nickelodeon, were still up.

As Jack slapped glue onto a fence, Guard Uncle walked up.

"Hey, boy. Sorry about yesterday. I really came over to give you this!" He pulled out a dollar. "For you from Cat Uncle. He's out of jail and asked me to give you this for your work the other night. And here's an extra dime."

"What for?" Jack was suspicious.

"The doorman always gives the errand boy some tea money, didn't you know?" Guard Uncle chuckled. "It's for good luck, for both you and me."

"Thank you!"

"How did you escape without being arrested?"

"I hid under the floorboards in the storage room."

"But how did you know they were loose?"

"Just lucky, I guess. Hey Guard Uncle, have you eaten?"

"Going home to cook now!" He lifted a chunk of fresh meat, hanging from a string. "No fancy restaurant food for me in the next while."

Guard Uncle didn't wear a pigtail like most of Chinatown's men. He had a shock of short white hair that bristled like a brush.

"Has Cat Uncle decided when he will reopen?" asked Jack.

"You ask him!" The old man cursed and spat. "You two are related."

"Guard Uncle, you know everything," Jack said, trying to butter him up. "Did you know his servant girl Mei?"

"The one who ran away?" Guard Uncle's face seemed to soften as he recalled her. "I saw her a few times. I often wonder where she is now."

"Why did she run away?"

"Your aunty complained that the girl was lazy, but I think she had dreams for a better life. She loved to sing, even while she was scrubbing the floor or chopping firewood. Your uncle praised her for taking good care of your aunty. She was very bright too, and I think your uncle started to teach her how to read and write." Guard Uncle grinned. "Do you fancy her? Isn't she a bit too old for you?"

Jack ignored the tease and pressed on. "Does she have family here?"

Guard Uncle shut his eyes to think. "What was her name? Something Mei. Mei, Mei, Mei . . . Ah, I remember. So-mei. Liu So-mei. I knew a girl back home with a similar name. Oh well, time to go home and cook," he said, walking away.

Good thing I went to work for Cat Uncle, Jack thought, putting the money in his safest pocket.

As Jack walked down the hall toward his apartment, he could hear Cat Aunty's loud voice. "Do you want to destroy me?"

"You must tell him the truth. You can't send him off to China. That won't solve anything!" Ma replied.

"Quiet! You want the neighbours to hear?" Cat Aunty said, lowering her voice.

Jack braced himself and walked in.

Cat Aunty smiled at him. She was serving tea in fine china cups to his mother.

"We saved this for you," Ma said, handing him a plate of crackers, each covered in sweet condensed milk.

"Thanks," Jack said.

"Your mother wasn't feeling well, so I came over," Cat Aunty said, standing up to brush crumbs from her smock. "But she's all cheered up now. I have to go. There's still a lot of packing left to do before Kern leaves. Are you coming to the docks to say goodbye to him?"

"Of course."

"Thank you for the flowers," Ma said.

Three small pots with flowering geraniums lay on the table.

"Tomorrow I'll bring Dolly Aunty to you," Cat Aunty replied. "You need some help around here."

After the door closed, Ma busied herself with the dishes. "Your aunty stayed all afternoon! I had two buckets of clothes to scrub and a rush job of feather-stitching to do. But instead I had to sit and chat with her."

"Why did she bring this?" asked Jack, pointing to the plants. "She knows we don't get enough sunlight here."

"She says plants bring life to a room," Ma replied.

"What's this?" Jack asked, picking up a sheet of paper covered with fancy brushwork. It was just like the ones he'd seen at Cat Aunty's home.

"It's an anti-ghost charm."

"You told her about last night?"

"The entire building knows, so she brought me one of her anti-ghost charms. Go stick it on the front door."

"Just now, were you and Cat Aunty talking about Kern?"

"How dare you eavesdrop!" Ma's eyes flashed with anger. "You have no respect. Go put that charm up—right now!"

"You know that Kern doesn't want to go to China, don't you?"

Ma turned away without answering.

He took the charm and a pot of glue into the hallway and shut the door.

Temple Keeper wasn't able to chase the ghost away from

the nickelodeon, he thought. *So will his paper charms work here? I'm sure the ghost girl at the nickelodeon is Liu So-mei, but everyone says she ran away to the Chinese Mission. What really happened to her?*

"Jack, I'm glad I caught you," William Uncle called out.

Jack was surprised to see him here.

"When is the nickelodeon reopening?" asked the piano man.

"Haven't you seen the posters? I spent all afternoon putting them up all over Chinatown."

"I never read those posters. They just want me to spend money on useless things."

"We reopen on Sunday. The Chinese consul is coming!"

"But that's my day for church."

"Then come after church. William Uncle, I need to know about the Chinese Mission."

When William Uncle gave him a puzzled look, Jack said, "I never heard about it until today!"

"That's where the missionary ladies rescued runaway slave girls and servants who had been mistreated by their owners. The church women taught the girls English and practical skills like sewing, and sent them out into the world to lead decent lives. But the earthquake fire destroyed the mission. Now it's on the other side of the bay, in Oakland. As a matter of fact, my church is raising money to rebuild the mission."

"Will your pastor know about the girls who lived there?"

"No, but the one at the Presbyterian Church on Stockton Street will know something."

After William Uncle left, Jack was stuck with one worry. *Will the pastor bother to help someone like me?*

There were as many churches as there were temples in Chinatown. The Presbyterian congregation met in a long low shed, a temporary building that would serve them until their new hall was built.

Jack stepped inside. The walls were bare except for a large cross of polished wood. Hymns were written on blackboards, in Chinese and English. There was no piano. *I don't belong here. I'm not a Christian.* Jack swallowed hard. *Worse, I'm going to tell a lie to a man of God!*

But he had no choice. He wished William Uncle were with him. Jack rubbed his damp palms on his trousers and called out, "Is someone here?"

The pastor hurried out, smiling. His fingers were smudged with blue ink.

"Sir, here are some plants," Jack said, pulling Cat Aunty's plants out of a sack and placing them on a nearby table. Miraculously, none of the pots were broken. Some clumps of soil had spilled out, and he quickly swept them back into the pots. "They can be sold to raise money for your new building."

"Thank you, you have a good heart. What is your surname?"

When Jack told him, the pastor said, "Ah yes, I have heard about your family. Your mother is a widow and has two daughters, does she not?"

Jack nodded.

"Your mother should bring your family to church here. She will get much help and comfort from the word of God."

"I have a question, sir," Jack blurted out. "How would I find out if a girl from Chinatown ran away to the Chinese Mission?"

The pastor's moustache twitched. "You would look at the records of the Chinese Mission."

"They weren't burned in the fire?"

"No, the matron risked her life to save them. Soldiers almost shot her when she went back to the building. They thought she was a looter!"

Jack took a deep breath. "Sir, my mother's sister Liu Somei came here eighteen years ago to work as a servant. Now my mother can't find her."

"I arrived in 1900, so I don't know about what happened before I came here."

"Sir, could you find out for me?"

"But that's a lot of work."

"If you help my mother, then I'm sure she will bring her daughters here."

"Ah, that would be good." The pastor beamed. "Are you a Christian?"

"My brother and I went to church near Marysville for a while. But then we stopped."

"Why?"

"The people there didn't want Chinese in their church."

"Not all people are like that. Let me see if I can get a telephone call through to Oakland. The woman arrived eighteen years ago, is that right?"

"Yes."

"I'll be right back," the pastor said, going into the backroom.

Jack went to the window and looked outside. One of Chinatown's last cigar factories used to be on this street.

Sometimes Cat Uncle gave him a nickel to run over there to pick up a box for him. The factory smelled heavenly.

He sat down, opened a Bible, stuck his finger on a passage and read: "A false witness will not go unpunished, and he who breathes out lies will perish."

It's a good thing I'm not a Christian, thought Jack, *or I'd be in deep trouble.*

Just then the pastor returned. "I see you're reading the Bible. Good for you. I truly wish I could help your mother, but unfortunately the Chinese Mission has absolutely no record of a girl named Liu So-mei."

Cat Aunty's story isn't true! A dead end!

"Thank you for your help, sir. We'll be sure to come to church on Sunday."

CHAPTER NINE

Thursday, Late Afternoon

As Jack rounded the corner near the church, he saw Yu-yi crossing the road with a basket of fresh vegetables. She had her head down and was stepping carefully through the mud and horse manure.

Suddenly a horse and wagon shot out from a side lane, heading straight for her.

The driver yanked his reins, and the horse reared up in front of Yu-yi, kicking its front legs in the air above her. The horse whinnied shrilly, its hooves inches from her forehead.

"Yahhh!" Yu-yi fell and tried to crawl away. But the bucking horse loomed over her.

"Piper, easy! Down, boy, down!" the driver shouted. The horse's eyes bulged from their sockets.

Jack sprinted over and pulled Yu-yi away. They ran to the other side of the street.

"Get that animal down!" Another driver ran to the wagon, jumping and trying to grab for the horse's collar.

Piper's owner braced himself against the footboard, using every ounce of strength to rein in the horse. Finally the animal settled down, snorting and pawing restlessly.

"Something spooked Piper," the driver told the second man. "All of a sudden he was out of control. I don't know what it was. I've never seen him like this!"

"Are you all right?" Jack asked Yu-yi.

She slid to the ground and started to whimper, hugging herself tightly.

"You're safe now," he said. "Don't be scared."

"It . . . it's . . . it's Lincoln," she stuttered, her eyes wide with fear. "The anti-ghost charm you gave me doesn't work." Yu-yi swallowed hard. "He still wants me to join him in the world of the dead. He wants me for his ghost bride. He's trying to kill me!"

"Kill you?" Jack sputtered in shock. "Lincoln would never do that. If he caused your death, you would never agree to be his bride in the ghost world."

"Oh, Jack, please help me. I don't want to be a ghost bride, and I don't want to marry Old Kong!"

"No, of course you don't. Of course you don't." Over her shoulder he saw Lincoln standing in the shadows, hunched over, looking hurt and bewildered. Then his brother held up one hand as if to ask "Why?" Jack gulped and shivered. He felt both angry and sad. His brother had become more of a stranger than ever before. Jack opened his mouth, but no words came out.

Then Lincoln vanished.

"Yu-yi, don't worry," Jack said. "I won't let Lincoln hurt you."

"Thank you," Yu-yi said. She smiled and brushed off the mud clinging to her. "You're saving my life."

At night the darkened temple looked even more imposing and fearful. Only the candles inside hinted at safety and warmth. Jack wished that more of them had been lit.

"Temple Keeper, where are you?" Jack called out. He shuddered from the cold. Outside and far away, a dog barked ferociously.

"Youngster, this had better be important," Temple Keeper growled. "I fell asleep just a moment ago. I've been at the cemetery the entire day unearthing bones. My back hurts."

In the candlelight, Jack could barely make out Temple Keeper's face. "Sir, is it possible," he asked, "that a ghost would kill a girl in order to make her his ghost bride?"

"Why do you ask?"

"Because Lincoln's ghost wants Yu-yi for his bride."

"No ghost would ever kill anyone in order to get a bride. Spirits aren't stupid. They know the soul of any person murdered by a ghost would never consent to be their bride. Tell that girl Yu-yi to stop worrying."

Jack felt his body sag with relief.

"Sir, is it possible that the ghost you caught in the hall could have escaped?"

"Not likely, but not impossible. Why do you ask?"

"My mother says she saw a female ghost in a mirror at home."

"That is entirely possible. I removed the ghost from your movie hall, and it will not return there. But there is no telling where it might go next."

"Sir, do you know anything about a servant girl named Liu So-mei?"

"Never heard such a name."

"I'm sure that's the ghost that scared everyone at the nickelodeon. Now I need to know what she wants! What can I do to find out?"

"You, you cannot do anything!" Temple Keeper snorted. "You are just a boy, what do you know? Listen to me: communication is not easy between the living and dead. Ghosts are like flashes of lightning. They have no solid form, and we glimpse them only briefly. We fear them because we do not understand them. But we should not fear them at all. They are not all-powerful. Otherwise they would rule the world of the living!"

"Sir, what happens when we send ghosts meat and drinks? Doesn't that food give them a solid form?"

"No, those offerings are just ways we show our respect. Only one thing can help a ghost become more material . . ." Temple Keeper stopped abruptly. "But it is too dangerous! And you are too young to hear such things."

"I'm the man in my family now. My mother depends on me!"

"You're still a boy!"

"I won't leave until you tell me. I'll sit here all night."

"Go home, youngster. It's getting late."

Jack refused to move.

Temple Keeper walked back and forth impatiently, one hand massaging his back. He shook his head and muttered to himself. Finally he sighed and spoke. "If someone from the living world invited a ghost from the other world to come over, then that ghost would have a stronger presence here. But it is rarely done, and too dangerous."

Jack gulped.

Temple Keeper continued. "The danger is that once you bring over a ghost, there's no guarantee that it will go back. It is the same as if you invite people into your home. It is easy to ask them in, but if they don't want to leave, then you have a big problem."

I don't care. I have to try something.

The stores of Chinatown were still open, doing a brisk trade with customers. Shopkeepers dangled light bulbs over their storefronts to help brighten the streets. But the wind, bringing in a Pacific storm, swung the electric cords back and forth and cast ghostly, moving shadows along the walls and streets. Under wide awnings, energetic clerks shouted out the day's best bargains. Restaurants and noodle houses were crowded with noisy customers.

At a dry-goods store, Jack pulled out Guard Uncle's dollar bill and stared longingly at it before buying candles, incense and a packet of spirit money. He also asked the clerk to use brush and black ink to write Lincoln and So-mei's names in Chinese on two sheets of paper.

This was Jack's first time entering the nickelodeon by himself at night.

"Anyone here?" he called.

Edging his way into the pitch-black interior, he groped for the light switch. When the lights came on, he breathed more easily. Quickly, he glued the sheets with the two names on a wall, just above the floor. He fetched two cups of leftover tea from the thermos flask. He lit the incense and candles, planting them in a can of soil. He put his hands together and bowed three times to the names. Then he knelt and touched his head to the floor three times. He lit the spirit money, one sheet at a time, and dropped them into a bucket. The ashes swirled around and flew over his head, propelled by the heat of the flames. This was what they did at home, on Ba's birth and death days.

"So-mei Elder Sister?" His voice quivered. "So-mei Elder Sister, are you here? So-mei Elder Sister, I burned spirit money and I brought you food and drink. I hope you will accept them. I know you have unfinished business here. I will help you in any way I can. But you must tell me what it is you want!"

He glanced around the hall. Outside, a stray cat mewed and startled Jack.

"Please, So-mei Elder Sister, talk to me."

After a while he called out, "Lincoln Elder Brother, are you here? Listen, Yu-yi is afraid of you. Leave her alone, all right? Show yourself to me. I have yin-yang eyes."

He sat back and watched the candlelight flicker. For most of his life, he had turned away whenever he saw a ghost. They had never harmed him, yet he was afraid of them. And here he was, begging two ghosts to reveal themselves.

A sudden thought jolted him. *Two ghosts, Lincoln and So-mei. Lincoln is a good person; maybe So-mei will like him. And So-mei is pretty. Maybe Lincoln will like her.*

Jack took the two candles and placed one in front of each name sheet. Then he bowed three times, took both candles and tilted them so that the two flames merged.

"Liu So-mei, this is Lincoln Leong. Lincoln Leong, this is Liu So-mei."

Just then the door flew open. It was Kern. Jack quickly ripped the sheets off the wall and stuffed them into his pocket.

"Hey, I've been looking for you," Kern said.

"I've been looking for you too. Your mother and mine are keeping a secret from you."

"What?"

"I don't know, but it has to do with you being sent to China."

"What's all this?" Kern asked, pointing to the candles. "You're doing something weird here, aren't you? Didn't Temple Keeper drive that ghost away?"

"No."

"No?" Kern seemed surprised. "How do you know?"

"I saw her here, after Temple Keeper said he'd caught her."

"What, you can see ghosts?"

Jack took a deep breath and said, "I have yin-yang eyes."

Kern turned away. "Let's get out of here."

"Wait, will you?" Jack called out. Then he lowered his voice. "There are ghosts here."

"Ghosts? There's more than one?"

"Lincoln is back, and the other is Mei, your mother's servant girl."

"You're crazy!" Kern bolted for the door. "You don't know what you're talking about."

"Remember that old photograph of your parents?"

"Yes, so?"

"Gee Uncle said the outhouse was haunted."

"So what? Mother said the same thing. She never believed those stories. She wasn't afraid of the backyard. She planted flowers there and was always busy watering and fertilizing, digging and moving plants. Listen, Mother's going out tomorrow afternoon. Want to try again?"

"Try what?"

"Try to get some money!" Kern stuck out his hand as if holding a key, and twisted it around and around.

So-mei's spirit suddenly appeared, arms stretched out, baggy sleeves hanging as if soaking wet.

"Yikes! A ghost!" Jack screamed.

"Where?"

"Behind you! At the window! Watch out, she's coming right at you!"

The ghostly form seemed to be gliding on wheels.

"No ghost can get to me!" Kern declared. He ducked and pulled a charm out from under his shirt. "Ma gave me this when I was little and told me to never take it off."

Jack watched, astounded, as So-mei's shape approached Kern. Then it broke up and faded away. But she reappeared near the back door. She looked as if she was weeping. Then she passed through the solid wood door.

"It's going into the backyard!" Jack shouted. "Come on!"

They ran to the door and yanked it open.

A faint yellow light flickered in the backyard over the jungle of bushy plants, tall grasses and weeds. The moon threw shadows across the yard. A strong wind blew through the trees and slammed the outhouse door shut with a loud bang.

"She's standing right there in front of the outhouse," Jack whispered.

"I don't see anything. What's she doing?"

"Her hand is pointing down. Yikes!"

"What happened?"

Jack's mouth hung open, his eyes wide from disbelief.

"What happened?" Kern asked again. "Tell me!"

"She dove into the ground and disappeared!"

CHAPTER TEN

Friday Afternoon

I t was raining hard and Jack was soaked by the time he got home from school. His feet were wet too from a crack in the sole of his shoe. Two large umbrellas dripped water into a bucket at his front door.

"Jackson, say hello to Dolly Aunty," Cat Aunty called out. "You don't know her, but her husband owns Daw Lee, on Heaven Empress Temple Street. Her English name comes from their store."

"Hello, Dolly Aunty," Jack said, forcing himself to smile.

The three women were in the kitchen, sitting around the table with teacups and plates of fancy sweets. Jack looked for crackers with condensed milk, but he didn't see any.

Dolly Aunty was shorter and much older than both Ma and Cat Aunty, but stout and strong. Her Chinese smock and trousers were bordered with bright bands of embroidered cloth. She wore her grey hair pulled into a bun, fastened in place by fancy silver hairpins. The light glinted on her eyeglasses.

She reached out and grasped Jack's hands.

"What a handsome boy!" she exclaimed.

He pulled away. He hated having ladies fuss over him.

"His face has wonderful features," she said, continuing. "His forehead is broad—that means he is wise and smart. His jaw is firm—that means he is determined but not stubborn. And his ears are big, which means he has a long life ahead."

Jack's face turned red.

"Big ears are good? Hah!" Ma snorted. "Only for snooping!" Then she twisted one of his ears, hard.

"Ow!" Jack hollered. "Let go!"

"Jack's a good boy," Cat Aunty said, "and a hard worker. He's been running the nickelodeon, and he even worked for my husband. How I wish my Kern was more like Jack. In fact, the other night Jack was the only one to escape from the police raid!"

"You are well protected by the gods!" Dolly Aunty smiled. "How did you get away?"

Jack described how he hid under the floorboards. To shock the ladies, he made up a story about how a huge pack of rats had scampered by him.

"Guard Uncle told me all about your escape!" Cat Aunty said. "The judge released him long before he let my husband go."

"Guard Uncle wore a pigtail once," Dolly Aunty said, turning to Jack. "One day he came to me asking if I could find him a wife. He thought I would let him marry one of my servant girls." She laughed. "I told him, 'Earn more money first! And go fix your teeth!'"

Jack grinned. "Need more hot water for your tea?" he asked. He went to the sink to fill the kettle.

"What a helpful lad you are!" Dolly Aunty exclaimed, switching to English. She spoke with only a slight accent.

"You speak English!" Jack exclaimed.

"Only a little bit."

"Oh, she's being modest," Cat Aunty said. "She speaks excellent English. She learned to read and write from the church missionaries."

"They were the best teachers," Dolly Aunty said. "They became my long-time friends as well."

Jack waited by the stove for the water to heat up.

"Dolly has many skills," Cat Aunty said to Ma in a low voice. "She was a midwife. For years, her record was the best. Most of the babies delivered by her hands survived their birth and grew up. And the mothers whom she looked after, they also lived long past the birthing!"

"I also brought homeless and abandoned girls from China to America," Dolly Aunty announced. "I found good homes for the young pretty ones and jobs as servants and nannies for the other girls, until they were old enough to be married off."

"Dolly Aunty," Jack interrupted as he carried hot water to the table. "Did you help a girl named Liu So-mei?"

The room fell silent. The women stiffened and looked at one another.

"You are so enterprising," Ma said to Dolly Aunty. "Did you earn much money from bringing those girls here?"

"How could I? The laws of this country only allowed me to bring in two or three Chinese girls a year."

"But look at you!" Ma exclaimed. "You wear silver and jade and gold. Your husband must be rich!"

"Hah! Our store is so small, we have only one clerk! If my old fool was better at business, then I would have stayed home. Who wants to go into the fog and rain to work? Look at these hands. They are worn from hard labour and hot water."

"It's time for us to go," Cat Aunty said, standing up and glancing at her watch.

"Thank you, Dolly, for helping me with my medicine," Ma said.

After the visitors left, Jack rinsed the teacups and spoons. The girls ran in and grabbed the remaining cookies and sweet tarts. Ma hurried into the sitting room, to the window with the most daylight. Someone had dropped off a stack of new vests. She used a needle to pull out the white basting threads.

"Kitchen is all clean," Jack said, joining Ma in the sitting room. He shooed his sisters away because they were dropping crumbs on the piecework.

"Do you know what that woman wanted?" she whispered. "She wanted me to let her arrange for Anna to be sold as a servant. She said there are plenty of rich families who would pay a lot for her."

"You wouldn't do that, would you?"

"Did I say I would?"

Jack spotted Dolly Aunty's eyeglass case on the kitchen

table. He went over and slipped it into his pocket. "I'm going to meet Kern!" he said.

"Take an umbrella!" Ma called out.

But Jack was in such a hurry that he ran straight into the pouring rain.

Heaven Empress Temple Street, also known as Waverly Place, boasted the first permanent building in Chinatown after the earthquake. A powerful home-country club had raised money to put up the four-storey brick structure along with fancy ironwork and plate glass windows. The flags of the United States and China hung from tall poles mounted high above the roof. Next door to this grand-looking building, the Daw Lee store looked flimsy.

"I'm looking for Dolly Aunty," Jack said to a clerk who was tallying receipts using an abacus.

"Who are you?"

"Your boss lady was visiting my mother." Jack brandished the eyeglass case. "She forgot to take this."

"Leave it here." The man flicked the abacus beads at high speed.

"My mother said to hand it to her personally."

Annoyed, the clerk rolled his eyes and pointed to the stairs.

Jack ran up and stopped in front of the door. There was an anti-ghost charm on it, just like the one Cat Aunty had given Ma. He knocked.

"Who is it?"

"Jackson Leong!"

"Come in!"

As Jack entered, he saw Dolly Aunty slip a stack of ten-dollar bills into the drawer of her desk.

"Dolly Aunty, here's your eyeglass case. You left it in our house."

"Oh, look at you! Soaking wet! I'll get you a cloth."

She hurried off as Jack wiped the rain from his face and looked around. The room contained several sets of Chinese-style chairs made of hard polished wood with no padding. Long scrolls of calligraphy hung on the walls. A porcelain vase in a corner of the room stood almost as tall as him. Across from it was a bookcase, filled with bound volumes, little statues and small picture frames.

Dolly Aunty returned and handed him a towel. "Dry your hair thoroughly. You must not catch a cold."

"Thank you," said Jack, taking it.

"Hey, boss lady, telephone call!" the clerk shouted from downstairs.

"Coming!" she replied and turned to Jack. "I'll be right back."

Jack dropped the towel and went to the desk, where he spotted a pile of notebooks. He opened the top one and flipped through it. It was a detailed record of Dolly Aunty's income and expenses. As he turned the pages, he came to Liu So-mei's name. His hands started to shake, but before he could take a closer look, he heard Dolly Aunty coming up the stairs. He slammed the notebook shut just before she came in.

"That was Madame Fung. Her stupid servant girl Yu-yi is refusing to marry your landlord," Dolly Aunty said.

"Some people think Old Kong is too old for her."

Dolly Aunty gave him a tight smile. "You'd better hurry home."

She opened the door. As Jack went through, he pointed to the charm. "Who is this protecting you against?"

"Thank you for bringing my eyeglasses back." Dolly Aunty tried to shut the door, but Jack blocked it with his foot.

"That's to protect you from Liu So-mei's ghost, isn't it?" he asked.

"Who?"

"Liu So-mei."

Dolly Aunty pushed at the door but couldn't budge it. "Why are you so interested in her?"

"Her ghost came and scared Ma, and I need to know what she wants."

"All I did was arrange for her to work for Cat Aunty. Now go, before I call my clerk to kick you out!"

Jack darted through heavy rain, past building sites. When rain descended on the city, horse manure melted into the deep puddles on every street. A horse pulling an empty wagon galloped by. The driver cracked his whip. The wheels splashed through a puddle, drenching Jack's jacket, shirt and face. He shouted angrily and spat out the foul-tasting water. But the driver was long gone.

The street was littered with Old Bread-face's posters, which had been washed away in the rain.

What a waste of my afternoon. What a waste of our money.

By the time Jack knocked at Kern's door, he had come up with a plan.

Cat Uncle threw open the door. He was wearing pyjamas and holding the day's newspapers. He rolled the newspaper into a tube and rapped Jack's head. "Why are you banging at the door so late?" he shouted.

"Cat Uncle, when do you reopen your shop?"

"Don't know yet." He yawned. "Maybe it's time to change my line of business. That would make your mother happy, wouldn't it?"

"Is Kern here? Is he packing?"

"He's on the third floor. Old Kong came by and evicted Big Ear Mar and his no-good nephew. They ran out of time to pay their rent."

Jack gulped. His family might be next to get thrown out.

"Old Kong is paying Kern to carry all of their furniture down to the street."

"I'll go help him," Jack offered.

When he walked into apartment 305, Kern was emptying drawers onto the floor. Cupboards were open, chairs were overturned. Everything was topsy-turvy.

"There's nothing worth money here," Kern grumbled. "I thought I'd find something to sell."

"Listen, I know where you can get some money," Jack said. "Where?"

"Dolly Aunty's apartment."

"You're crazy!"

"I just came from there, and I saw a pile of cash in her desk. We just need a way to get in when no one is home."

Kern grinned. "We're lucky eggs! Dolly Aunty and my

106

mother are going to the temple tomorrow morning, to pray for a safe voyage for me. So the coast will be clear. I'll think of a plan to get in there."

"Done."

Kern gave him a funny look. "How come you're helping me now? Before, you backed off every time."

"We're cousins! We stick together!"

They shook hands vigorously.

"Shall we move the furniture down to the street now?"

"Just don't drop anything heavy on me."

CHAPTER ELEVEN

Saturday Morning

All morning Jack waited for Kern. He could hardly sit still, but he had to help Ma with the sewing. Several more bundles of vests had arrived from the jobber, and the crisp smell of fresh cloth filled the room.

As Jack wondered what sort of plan Kern had for getting them into Dolly Aunty's place, a bundle of soft cloth slipped through his hands and fell to the floor.

"Watch what you're doing!" Ma said. "That's Charlotte Fong's sister's wedding dress. I'm putting in the button holes. Is Charlotte wearing red colours now?"

"Yes, how did you know?"

"Because when a girl gets married, her sisters wear red to celebrate."

"I overheard Charlotte say that her parents went to a

matchmaker to choose a husband for her sister. Would you have done that for Lincoln?"

"I wouldn't have needed to. He was the best catch in all of California!"

She and Jack burst out laughing—something they had not done in a long time. Ma laughed so hard her eyes started to water and she pulled out a handkerchief from her pocket. It was Lincoln's birthday handkerchief. He wondered for a moment if he should tell her about Yu-yi's encounter with the horse and her fear that the anti-ghost charm wasn't working. But Jack didn't want to disturb Ma's cheery mood. He would handle the matter of Lincoln's ghost himself.

After Ma put the handkerchief back in her pocket, Jack asked, "Will I have to have an arranged marriage too?"

"Of course, but you're too young to worry about that."

I wouldn't mind an arranged marriage with Yu-yi, Jack thought.

Just then there was a knock at the door. Anna ran to open it and Kern rushed in. He stopped and took off his cap to greet Ma. Then he called out hello to Anna, who stood at the door looking hurt.

"Finished packing yet?" Ma called out.

"Almost," Kern said, shooting a knowing glance at Jack. "Mother is fussing."

"Parents are like that!" Ma exclaimed.

"Let's go," Jack said, grabbing his jacket.

"Don't stay out too long, Jack," she called out. "We still have to finish the vests."

"Let me see your anti-ghost charm," Jack whispered to Kern.

He handed it over.

Jack untied the pouch, removed the tiny roll of cloth and shook it open.

"What's going on?" Kern asked.

"It's exactly the same as the one that Cat Aunty gave Ma and is on Dolly Aunty's door. It protects against Liu So-mei's ghost."

"Why?"

"I don't know."

The two boys ran down the stairs and out into the street. The rain had finally stopped but the skies were a dark grey.

"We'd better hurry," Kern said. "They'll only be at the temple for a little while."

"What about Dolly Uncle? Won't he still be at home?"

"He's escorting the ladies to the temple. It's perfect timing."

"Why didn't you come earlier? Then we would've had more time."

Kern stopped and confronted Jack. "Because I had to get this." He pulled a key from his pocket and waved it at Jack. "It opens the door to Dolly Aunty's apartment. How did you think we were going to get in there? People lock their doors, you dumb ox. There are thieves everywhere."

"Where'd you get it?" asked Jack, as they dodged pedestrians on the crowded street. "How do you get keys to so many places?"

"Same source! When Dolly Uncle moved into his new building, he asked Old Kong to install the locks to his apartment. I'm sure Old Kong's master key will open that door too."

When they turned the corner and saw the Daw Lee store,

Kern said, "Good. The shutters are up."

Every morning, store clerks removed the floor-to-ceiling shutter planks that protected the shops at night. The doors and counter windows were then left open to display the store's wares and to encourage customers to come in and browse.

"I was worried. Sometimes when it rains, the clerk at Daw Lee leaves the shutters down. That would have made it harder for us to get upstairs," Kern said.

"Now what?"

"I'm going to pretend to be buying some things I need for my trip. I'll look around the shop, talk to the clerk and get him away from the stairs. After a few minutes, you sneak upstairs and get the money. Here's the key."

Jack managed to get upstairs exactly as planned. He hurried to the desk, but the notebook wasn't there. He opened the drawer, saw the stack of bills and took four off the top.

She won't miss them.

Then he opened the other drawers. In the bottom one, he found the notebook. He stuffed it under his shirt and went back downstairs.

Kern was waiting for him at the door, holding his purchases neatly wrapped in brown paper.

Jack breathed a sigh of relief.

"Did you get the money?" Kern asked.

"Here." Jack handed him the bills.

"Thanks. This'll last me a long time in Marysville. Come on. I'll treat you to some noodles."

"You should save your money."

"Come on!"

As soon as they sat down at Golden Chrysanthemum Garden, Jack shoved the dirty dishes aside and wiped the table clean with his shirt sleeve. Then he opened the notebook. It was a record of income and expenses for placing servant girls, arranging adoptions and delivering babies. He quickly flipped through the pages until he came to the year 1893, where he had seen So-mei's name.

INCOME	EXPENSES	
March 20, 1893· Chy Lung & Company	Purchase:	$21·00
Servant girl: Suey Ching, $90·00	Ship passage:	$33·00
640 Sacramento St·, San Francisco	Translator:	$20·00
	Doctor Li Po Tai:	$5·00
	Total:	$79·00
April 11, 1893· Mrs· Hung Sang Lung	Birth registration:	$5·00
Birth of son: Mun Soon, $25·00		
206 Dupont St·, San Francisco		
June 6, 1893· Wing Fung Tai	Purchase:	$17·00
Servant girl: Oye Lan, $85·00	Ship passage:	$34·00
Webster Street, Oakland	Translator:	$20·00
	Doctor Li Po Tai:	$5·00
	Total:	$76·00
August 21, 1893· Mrs· Leong	Train fare:	$3·00
Birth of son: $30		
Marysville		
August 28, 1893· Servant So-mei		
Birth of son: $30		
Marysville		

"Look at this!" Jack said, showing Kern the notebook.

"Mei had a baby—so what?"

The waiter thumped down two bowls of barbecued pork noodles, and the boys grabbed their chopsticks.

"So that's why she ran away. She was having a baby in Marysville," Jack said, shovelling noodles into his mouth.

"Don't talk with your mouth full," Kern said, scooping up pork with his chopsticks and stuffing it into his mouth. "I'll bet your mother knows something about this. Give me that book."

Jack pushed the book toward Kern and continued eating.

"Look here—Dolly Aunty delivered Lincoln as well."

"They all know more about this than they're willing to tell."

"Now what?" Kern asked.

"We go to Temple Keeper. Mei's ghost is still lurking around, and we don't want her showing up at the opening of the nickelodeon tomorrow."

The temple doors were closed tight against the cold weather. They were heavy, and the hinges squealed as Jack and Kern pushed them open. No worshippers were there.

"Temple Keeper, sir, are you there?" Jack called out.

After a moment Temple Keeper walked out dressed in a padded gown. It reached to the floor and made him look larger than life. A woollen scarf was wrapped around his neck.

"Hey, boy, come back again?" Temple Keeper said in a sing-song voice. "You brought a friend this time. You have more tough questions for me?"

"Yes, sir, I do."

"Go ahead, then." He strolled back and forth to keep himself warm.

"Sir, I need your help," Jack said.

"Why should I help you?" Temple Keeper stiffened.

"Because only you can get this ghost to tell me what she wants."

"People in the living world cannot tell those in the world of the dead what to do," Temple Keeper declared. "The two worlds are separate."

"But, sir, if I don't know why the ghost has come back here, then I can't help her get what she wants, and she will keep bothering us."

"Yes, unless I drive it away." Temple Keeper puffed out his chest. "That is exactly what I did with that ghost at the nickelodeon. That is what Old Bread-face paid me for."

"But whatever you did didn't work."

"How dare you be so impertinent!" Temple Keeper glared at Jack.

"Sir, I saw the ghost there, after you left."

"Hah!" Temple Keeper dismissed him with a wave of his hand. "You, you cannot see ghosts."

"Yes I can!"

Temple Keeper shook his head impatiently. "If that is so, boy, then why did you not tell Old Bread-face to ask for his money back?"

"Because if people learned that you couldn't drive out the ghost from our nickelodeon, then they would be too scared to come to our movies."

"Stop bothering me with your nonsense!" He pushed the boys toward the door. "Get out!"

"I do see ghosts," Jack declared, pushing back. "Just like you. The ghost in the nickelodeon was a female."

"Hah!" roared Temple Keeper. "*I* told you that. Give me some real proof!"

"The ghost you saw at the nickelodeon was wearing a blue Chinese smock decorated with shiny bands of black material. Her hair was neatly coiled in a bun behind her head. She had a pretty face, a small mouth and a pockmark on her cheekbone just under the left edge of her right eye."

Temple Keeper's jaw dropped. "So you do have yin-yang eyes!"

"Will you help me now?" asked Jack.

"You won't be able to afford it."

"How much?"

"Twenty dollars."

Jack gulped.

"Sir, think about this," Kern spoke up. "If the ghost appears tomorrow when the nickelodeon opens, everyone will know that you failed to drive it away. You will be finished as Temple Keeper. But if you help us, then you have a chance of keeping your reputation."

Temple Keeper thought it over

"Be at the nickelodeon at sundown," he growled. "That is the only time we can invite the ghost."

CHAPTER TWELVE

Saturday Evening

The nickelodeon was dark, lit by a single candle.

Temple Keeper emerged from the shadows. This time, he wore ordinary street clothes and a Western-style jacket. The table looked bare compared to the earlier ritual. Three tiny plates, meant for soy sauce, held bits of uncooked food: grains of rice, dried mushrooms and tofu sticks. Temple Keeper tugged the jade ring off his finger and placed it on an upside-down bowl. In front of the bowl, he put a bell next to a pair of tiny shoes made from stiff white paper. The last thing he put on the table was a pan of dark soil about two inches deep.

"Do not be scared. Stand to the side and keep quiet," he said to the boys. "I am going to summon the ghost, but my invitation does not mean that it has to cross over."

As Temple Keeper rang the bell and started chanting in a low voice, the boys backed into the shadows.

"How long will this take?" Kern whispered.

"Don't know," Jack replied.

Temple Keeper put down the bell, knelt and touched his forehead to the floor three times. He remained in that position and started chanting.

"So-mei, So-mei, follow this voice.
Cross over, cross over,
From darkness to light."

Temple Keeper stood up and paused for a moment. He rang the bell again before resuming chanting and walking around the table.

"So-mei, So-mei, follow my voice.
The universe grants you strength,
Cross over from darkness to light."

Temple Keeper chanted faster and faster, and soon Jack couldn't make out the words.

Temple Keeper dropped to his knees and touched his forehead to the ground. When he stood up, he rang the bell for a third time.

"I don't think this is working," Kern whispered.

"Give him time," Jack retorted. "Sacred things often come in sets of three."

Temple Keeper swayed back and forth and chanted some more.

"Look!" Kern gasped. "The jade ring is glowing!"

The tiny circle of green stone brightened and darkened in a steady beat.

"Wow!" Jack's mouth dropped open. "The ring must be an opening between the world of the dead and the world of the living!"

The light around the ring faded and the solemn darkness seemed to deepen.

Temple Keeper came over to the boys, shaking his head. "I have done everything I can."

"Sir, don't we need some tea for the altar?" asked Jack. He remembered the liquid offerings from the first ritual.

"No."

The candle flickered and almost went out. Temple Keeper hurried over to protect the flame, cupping his hands around it.

So-mei appeared, floating over the altar. Temple Keeper stepped back when he saw her. In the low light, Jack saw only her face, pale and tinged with green. She bowed to Temple Keeper, who gravely returned the gesture. Then she exchanged bows with Jack.

"What's happening?" Kern asked anxiously. "Is it the ghost? Should I bow too?"

"Yes," Jack whispered. "She's bowing to you."

Kern obeyed, but So-mei darted to the back door just as she had done before.

"Let's follow her!" Jack said.

Kern followed Jack out the door and into the backyard. Temple Keeper joined them, carrying a lantern.

A gust of wind sprang up, and the sharp edges of flying

leaves snagged and scattered parts of Mei's form into the moonlit night. Somehow the ghost regenerated itself. But whenever Kern got close to her, So-mei's image faded and broke up. It reminded Jack of the times that the projector at the nickelodeon jammed. The film clicked through at the wrong speed so the actors faded in and out.

So-mei stopped at the same spot where she had disappeared before. She knelt and placed both hands on the ground. She remained there without moving. Gradually her form became more solid. Jack could see her ears, even make out the tips of her fingers.

"So-mei Elder Sister, speak," Jack pleaded. "Tell us what you want."

The ghost opened her mouth, and it looked as if she might say something. But no words came out. She made small circles over the ground with her hands. Then she vanished.

"Dig here," Temple Keeper said, pointing.

"What happened?" Kern asked, looking puzzled.

"She's gone," Temple Keeper said. "But I suspect she buried something here. There are tools leaning against the outhouse. Bring them here."

Jack brought over a pick and a shovel.

"Sir, why didn't So-mei speak to us?" he asked.

"It takes far too much energy for a ghost to speak. Just dig."

"But we need to find out what her unfinished business is," Jack insisted. "Otherwise all of this digging is useless."

"Be patient, boy."

Jack and Kern pulled up bushes and weeds and threw them to one side. Kern used the pick to loosen the soil, while Jack used the shovel to dig. Soon both boys were breathing hard and sweating. Once the roots were out of the way, the work moved along quickly.

"How deep do we go?" Jack asked. "Feels like we're digging a grave."

"Maybe we can get jobs as gravediggers," Kern muttered.

"Stop talking nonsense and dig," Temple Keeper ordered.

In the distance a mournful dog howled.

"Maybe we should come back tomorrow in the daytime," Kern suggested.

"You're scared!" Temple Keeper chortled.

Jack's shovel struck metal. "I found something!" he shouted.

Temple Keeper hurried over and dipped the lantern into the hole.

Jack saw a long piece of smooth grey metal below. Kern went over and they scooped up the loose soil with their bare hands. The earth was cold and clammy, and the sides of the pit started to crumble.

Temple Keeper almost slipped and fell in. "Be careful!"

"I am being careful!" Kern snapped.

"What if it's a coffin?" Jack asked. "We're not going to stir up some angry ghost, are we?"

A stray cat suddenly yowled, and both of the boys jumped out of the hole.

"Get back there and finish the job, you spineless fools," Temple Keeper hissed.

The boys hopped back down and dug deeper, uncovering a tin box. It was tilted at a steep angle. They tried to move it, but there was no handle and their hands kept slipping off the smooth metal surface. Jack and Kern cursed in frustration.

Finally they managed to lift the box out of the hole. Then they saw that a padlock held the lid tightly in place.

Jack stood back while Kern swung the pick.

"Easy!" Temple Keeper cautioned. "Be careful."

Kern easily knocked the rusted padlock off. As Jack lifted the lid, a sweet musty odour engulfed them. It came from a large cloth-wrapped bundle that was crammed inside, the fabric knotted at the top.

Jack started to untie the knot, but the rotting cloth fell apart, revealing an ivory-coloured skull on top of a pile of bones. He gasped and fell back. But there was no time to be scared. He took a deep breath and slid his hands down along the sides of the box. At the bottom, a loop of string got caught on his finger. When he pulled it out a charm pouch dangled there, identical to the one that Kern wore around his neck.

CHAPTER THIRTEEN

Saturday Night

The two boys gently placed the box of bones in front of Kern's apartment and looked at one another.

"Shall we take that down?" Kern asked, pointing to the anti-ghost charm on the door.

"Yes," Jack said, ripping it off. "It's not helping anyone."

As they entered the apartment with the box, Cat Uncle stormed into the hallway.

"Stupid boy, where were you?" he shouted at Kern. "Your mother looked everywhere for you. She thought you had run away. She told me to go to the police station to report you missing!"

"We were at the nickelodeon," Kern said.

"What's that dirty box?" Cat Uncle asked. "Get rid of that before your mother sees it!"

One of the family cats crept up, sniffed at the box and streaked out the door.

"I've been holding up dinner for you!" Cat Aunty called from the kitchen. "I cooked all your favourite foods."

"That box is wet and will ruin the carpet," Cat Uncle muttered.

Cat Aunty gasped when she saw the container. She backed away, clutching the anti-ghost charm at her neck. She sank into a nearby chair.

"What's the matter? What's wrong?" Cat Uncle asked.

"Nothing," she said weakly, shaking her head.

"Aunty, what are you hiding?" Jack asked. "Don't make things worse."

"You know all about this, don't you?" Kern pointed an accusing finger at her.

"Don't talk to your mother like that," Cat Uncle said. "Just get that filthy box out of here!"

"Yes!" Cat Aunty cried out. "Get rid of it!"

"Not until I show you what's inside," Kern said.

When he lifted the lid, Cat Aunty covered her eyes and turned away. But Cat Uncle stepped up and looked inside.

"Bones. Human bones!" Kern declared. "And this ghost charm—" he waved it in front of his father's face, "—it's the same as the one that was on our door. Show him, Jack. And the same one that mother gave me and Dolly Aunty."

"And Ma too," Jack added, holding out the charm.

"What's this all about?" Cat Uncle asked, turning to his wife.

"None of your business," she replied. "It's all ancient history. I will not say a word, and no one can force me."

She glared so fiercely at Kern that he backed away.

Jack rushed up to her. "Aunty, you'd better tell us— otherwise we'll summon the ghost," he said.

"Hah, you haven't the power to do that," Cat Aunty scoffed. "Not with all these charms around."

"What ghost?" Cat Uncle asked.

"The ghost of your servant girl So-mei," Jack said. "These are her bones."

Cat Uncle staggered back, a look of disbelief on his face. He struggled to speak. "How . . . how do you know?" he stuttered. "I mean, do you . . . do you know that for sure?"

"Temple Keeper helped her come back from the other world, and she showed us where to dig for the bones," Kern said. "They were behind the nickelodeon! Where we used to live!"

"You told me that So-mei ran off to the Chinese Mission," Cat Uncle said, confronting his wife. "You said they found her a husband."

"Not so," said Jack. "I asked at the Chinese Mission, and they had no record of So-mei ever being there. Go ask the pastor of the Chinese Presbyterian Church. He wouldn't lie."

"What happened to her?" Cat Uncle asked, grabbing his wife's arm.

"Nothing! Nothing happened to her."

"Then why do you have so many ghost charms?" Jack asked.

"And why was the same charm inside the box of bones?" Kern asked. He ripped the one from his neck and held both in front of his father.

"You gave me the same one when I came back from China," Cat Uncle said, ripping a pouch from around his neck.

125

"Don't be foolish," Cat Aunty cried out. "Put those charms back on. Right now! Before something terrible happens to you both."

Instead, Cat Uncle reached over and snatched the pouch hanging from her neck. Then he darted to the wall and tore down the faded yellow sheets of paper covered with Chinese brushwork.

"Give me all of the charms," Cat Uncle demanded, holding out his hand.

The boys handed them over, and Cat Uncle strode into the kitchen. "I'm burning all this. Paper charms, cloth charms, pouches, everything. Liu So-mei's ghost can come here and do whatever she wants now."

He lifted the trivet on the stove and threw everything into the fire. In the next instant, a chilly gust of wind swept through the room.

Her ghost is here!

The electric lights flickered, and in the dim light Jack saw So-mei hovering in front of Cat Aunty. This time the ghost's form was solid and a fiery look burned in her eyes.

"So-mei is here, Cat Aunty, and she wants you to tell the truth!"

"You're lying. You don't have yin-yang eyes."

"So-mei has a pockmark on her cheekbone just under the left edge of her right eye," Jack said.

"Aiee!" Cat Aunty shrieked. "You have the gift, just like your mother, but you can't make me tell. I won't. I can't!"

Slowly, one after another, the light bulbs in every room flickered and went out.

"Where is she now?" Cat Aunty asked, her voice trembling.

Jack peered into the dark. "So-mei Elder Sister," he whispered. "Where are you?"

There was no response.

Then Ma burst through the front door, and all the lights suddenly came back on.

"What's going on?" Ma asked. She was carrying a covered dish of hot food.

"So-mei's ghost was just here," Jack said.

"I warned you!" Ma said to Cat Aunty. "I knew something would happen, sooner or later."

Cat Aunty was trembling, her face white with fear. Her arms flailed in front of her as if she were trying to keep the ghost away.

"I'll tell . . . I'll tell . . ." she stammered, backing up against the wall and pointing an accusing finger at her husband. "Fifteen years ago, shortly after you left for China, our servant girl So-mei told me she was pregnant with your child."

"Father!" Kern gasped.

"So I took her to Marysville," Cat Aunty continued, "because my sister had told me she needed help with her newborn baby, Lincoln. We stayed there while So-mei's belly grew bigger and bigger. When the time came, I called for Dolly Aunty to deliver her. I paid for the best help there was, but So-mei died in childbirth despite all of Dolly Aunty's efforts. Then I sent a letter to China, saying that I had given birth to a son, Kern."

"You lied to me all these years!" Cat Uncle exclaimed.

"You knew about this too," Jack said, pointing at his mother.

"I tried to get your aunt to tell the truth," Ma protested. "But she was too scared."

"I was afraid because I hadn't given you a child," Cat Aunty said, her voice shaking. "When you went back to China, I was certain that you would get yourself a second wife. But I knew you wouldn't do that if I gave you a son."

"You should have trusted me," Cat Uncle said.

"How could I when you had given So-mei a child?" Cat Aunty's eyes flashed with sudden anger. "You went behind my back, sneaking around like a thief! A man can have several wives. People would congratulate you and even admire you. But a woman can have only one husband and must depend on him for everything."

"She's right," Ma said, embracing her sister. "Men have all the power."

"I didn't do anything wrong," Cat Aunty insisted.

"You lied about my real mother," Kern said. "How could you?"

"Don't look at me like that! I have loved you all my life," Cat Aunty said.

"Kern, your birth mother died while giving you life," Ma said, putting a hand on his arm. "I was there. I saw it happen. Go ask Dolly Aunty."

"After So-mei died, I was afraid her ghost would want to be near you," Cat Aunty said, pointing to Kern. "So I put an anti-ghost charm on her bones to stop her ghost from rising up."

"The earthquake must have disturbed the charm," Jack said. "When we found the trunk, it was tilted. And when we opened it, the charm had dropped to the bottom."

"But how did the bones get to San Francisco?" Kern asked.

"Seven years after So-mei's death," Ma said, "all the Chinese bones in the Marysville cemetery were dug up to be sent back to China. So I brought her bones here, and we buried them behind the nickelodeon."

"I'm so sorry. I'm so sorry, but I never thought this would hurt any living person," Cat Aunty said. "So-mei's death was beyond my control. There, I've told you everything now."

"So-mei! Mother!" Kern wailed. "Please, let me see you."

The anguished plea startled Jack.

"So-mei Little Sister," Ma said, "what can we do to give you peace?"

"Come back, So-mei," Cat Uncle called out, running to the front door and opening it. "Come back, one last time, please."

He ran to the windows, lifting them open. "So-mei, you gave me the son that I always wanted, but you received no respect. How can we honour you now? Tell us, and we will do all that we can."

Everyone looked around at the open windows and the door. But there was no sign of her.

"You call her," Cat Uncle urged his wife.

"So-mei," Cat Aunty pleaded in a soft voice. "Please, forgive me. I meant you no harm. I've been a good mother to your son. Isn't that so, Kern?"

"This is why you're sending me to China, isn't it? Because you knew my real mother's ghost had risen from the dead."

"Yes, I convinced your father to send you away. I was so afraid of the ghost, I didn't know what else to do," Cat Aunty said. "I'm so ashamed."

"We're both at fault," Ma said. "We both have much to regret."

"So-mei, please forgive us," the two women softly chanted.

Still, nothing happened.

"Will we ever have peace?" Cat Uncle asked. "Can So-mei ever forgive us?"

"Maybe there's something else she wants," Jack said. "Maybe she has another reason for coming back—another truth that she wants revealed."

Everyone turned to look at him.

"Is there something that you're not telling us?" Ma asked.

"I saw her ghost several times," Jack said.

"You have yin-yang eyes?" Ma asked.

"He does," Cat Aunty confirmed.

Jack went over to Kern. "I have to tell them about the money we stole," he whispered. "Will that be all right?"

Kern nodded.

"We stole some money from Dolly Aunty this morning while you were at the temple praying for Kern's safe journey," said Jack.

"Why?" Cat Uncle demanded. "What for?"

"We gave you everything you ever wanted," Cat Aunty told Kern.

"I never wanted to go to China," Kern said. "I was planning to run away. I needed the money to survive."

"You don't have to go to China, son." Cat Uncle put an arm around Kern. "But you do have to go back to school and study hard."

"You disappoint me, Jackson," Ma said, shaking her head. "How dare you steal money from Dolly Aunty? You're nothing but a common thief!"

"He told the truth," Cat Uncle said. "That counts for a lot. And don't forget—he was trying to help his cousin."

One by one, the lights went off again.

Now what? Jack thought. *What more does Mei want?*

"Has So-mei come back again?" Cat Aunty asked.

Jack squinted into the darkness. "I don't see her."

When the lights came back on, Cat Uncle let out a choked sob. "Now I know what to do. We must put So-mei's name on the ancestral altar in our village in China. Then everyone will honour her as the rightful mother of our son, Kern."

"Yes," Cat Aunty said, nodding. "If she has a final resting place, then she won't be a wandering ghost."

"I'll send the bones to China," Cat Uncle said, "and have the clan elders make the arrangements right away."

Cat Aunty and Ma nodded to one another. Then suddenly Ma jumped up and shouted, "It's Lincoln's ghost hovering over the box of bones!"

Jack saw him too. Lincoln was dressed exactly the way he had been on the day of the earthquake. He waved at Ma and Jack, as if to say goodbye.

"Wait!" Ma called out, but Lincoln had already disappeared into the box of bones.

Then Jack went over to Ma. "Give me Lincoln's handkerchief."

Ma pulled it from her blouse and handed it to him. He clutched it tightly for a second, then lifted up the lid on the box.

Everyone glanced at one another and gasped in alarm.

Then Jack placed the handkerchief on top of the bones and closed the lid.

Cat Aunty's two housecats ran up and rubbed their backs against the box, purring contentedly.

"Aie! It's So-mei and she's holding Lincoln's handkerchief!" Ma exclaimed.

"It's just as I'd hoped," Jack said. "Lincoln found himself a ghost bride!"

Then Lincoln rose up next to So-mei, took her hand in his and they vanished together.

"Let's change this farewell banquet into a wedding feast!" Jack said.

EPILOGUE

On Sunday afternoon a full house of paying customers filled every seat at the nickelodeon. Nothing disturbed the show, and the Chinese consul was very impressed. Ma paid Old Kong the back rent in full that afternoon. With Jack running the nickelodeon, she never had to worry again about money.

Kern returned the notebook and the money stolen from Dolly Aunty. He later became Chinatown's foremost carpenter.

When Madame Fung heard the story of how Lincoln's ghost wanted to save Yu-yi from a marriage with Old Kong, she cancelled the wedding.

Temple Keeper did not tell people about Jack's yin-yang eyes, which remained a family secret. From time to time, when Temple Keeper needed help with particularly devious ghosts, he would seek out Jack's help.

Books by PAUL YEE

Blood and Iron

Shu-Li and Diego

Learning to Fly

Shu-Li and Tamara

What Happened Last Summer

Chinatown: An Illustrated History...

Bamboo

A Song for Ba

The Bone Collector's Son

The Jade Necklace

Dead Man's Gold and Other Stories

Boy in the Attic

Ghost Train

Struggle and Hope

Breakaway

Roses Sing on New Snow

Tales from Gold Mountain

Saltwater City

The Curses of Third Uncle

Teach Me to Fly, Skyfighter!